SENSIBLE HOUSEKEEPER, SCANDALOUSLY PREGNANT

JENNIE LUCAS

~ Unexpected Babies ~

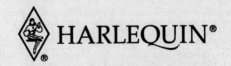

HARLEQUIN®

TORONTO • NEW YORK • LONDON
AMSTERDAM • PARIS • SYDNEY • HAMBURG
STOCKHOLM • ATHENS • TOKYO • MILAN • MADRID
PRAGUE • WARSAW • BUDAPEST • AUCKLAND

Recycling programs
for this product may
not exist in your area.

ISBN-13: 978-0-373-88160-4

SENSIBLE HOUSEKEEPER, SCANDALOUSLY PREGNANT

First North American Publication 2010.

Copyright © 2010 by Jennie Lucas.

www.eHarlequin.com

Printed in U.S.A.

SENSIBLE HOUSEKEEPER, SCANDALOUSLY PREGNANT

To Kimberley Young, the best editor in the world. Thanks for making my first ten books the best they could be!

CHAPTER ONE

THE gray sky dripped rain like mist, fine as cobwebs, across the dark minarets of Istanbul as Louisa Grey cut the last autumn roses from the garden. Her hands, usually so steady, trembled around her pruning scissors.

I can't be pregnant, she told herself fiercely. *Can't be!*

Could she…?

Abruptly Louisa sat back on her haunches, wiping her forehead with her sleeve in the cool twilight of early November. For a moment, she stared at the red and orange roses of the lush garden of the old Ottoman mansion. Then her hands fell into her lap. She felt the weight of the pruning shears against her gray woolen skirt.

Blinking fast, she turned her head blindly

to stare out at the red sunset shimmering across the Bosphorus.

One night. She'd worked for her ruthless playboy boss for five years. One night had ruined everything. She'd fled Paris the very next day, demanding a job transfer to his neglected home in Istanbul. She'd tried to put their night of passion behind her. But now, a month later, she had one terrified thought. One question that kept repeating itself in her mind. Every day, the question became louder and more afraid.

Could she be pregnant with her boss's baby?

"Miss? The cook's taken ill," a girl said in accented English behind her. "Please, may he go home?"

Louisa's shoulders instantly became steel-straight. Pushing her black-framed glasses up on her nose, she turned to face the young Turkish maid. She knew she must reveal no weakness to members of her staff who looked to her for leadership. "Why does he not ask me himself?"

"He's afraid you'll say no, miss. With so much to be done for Mr. Cruz's visit—"

"Mr. Cruz is not expected until the

morning of the dinner party. Tell the cook to go home. We will manage. But next time," Louisa added sharply, "he must ask me himself and not send someone else because he's afraid."

"Yes, miss."

"Also tell him he must be completely well by the day of the party, or he will be replaced."

With a timid movement like a curtsy, the maid departed.

Once Louisa was alone, her shoulders sagged. Leaning forward, she gathered two fallen roses from the grass and placed them in her basket. She picked up the pruning shears and rose heavily to her feet. She forced herself to go through the household checklist in her mind. The marble floors and chandeliers were sparkling clean. Her boss's favorite foods had been ordered to arrive fresh from the markets each day. His bedroom suite was ready, needing only these fresh roses to sweeten the dark, masculine room for whichever beautiful starlet he might choose to bring home with him this time.

Everything must be perfect for his visit. Mr. Cruz must have no reason whatsoever to complain. No reason, Louisa thought as she clipped the stem of the bush's very last rose with rather more force than necessary, to speak to her alone.

She heard the wrought-iron gate open with a long scraping sound behind her. She'd have to get that oiled, she thought. She turned, expecting to see the gardener, or perhaps the wine seller with the large delivery of champagne she'd ordered for the dinner party.

Instead she sucked in her breath as a towering figure stepped from the shadows. Except this man didn't just step out of the shadows.

He *was* the shadow.

"Mr. Cruz," she whispered, her mouth suddenly dry.

His eyes glittered in the twilight as he looked at her. "Miss Grey."

His deep, husky voice echoed across the garden, causing her heart to pound in her chest. She clenched her fingers tightly around the basket and pruning shears so her suddenly clumsy hands wouldn't drop them. He was three days early. But when had Rafael Cruz ever done what was expected?

Handsome, ruthless and rich, the

Argentinian millionaire had the darkly seductive charm of a poet—and a heart like ice.

Tall and broad-shouldered, with a latent power in his thickly muscled body, he stood out from all other men with his strength, his masculine beauty, his wealth and his stylish appearance. But today, his black hair was tousled. His usually immaculate black suit looked rumpled and his tie was loosened and askew at his neck. His jawline was dark with shadow below his sharp cheekbones and Roman nose. Light gray eyes stood out starkly against his tanned olive skin.

Disheveled as he was, today he looked barely civilized, half-brutal. And yet he was somehow even more handsome than she remembered.

A month ago, Louisa had been in his arms. For one night, he'd taken her body, he'd passionately taken her virginity—

She cut off the thought and took a deep, steadying breath.

"Good evening, sir." Her voice betrayed nothing of her emotion. It was dignified, almost cool—the perfect manner for the valued servant of a powerful man. Her training held her in good stead. "Welcome to Istanbul. Everything is in readiness for your visit."

"Of course." His lips curved into a sardonic smile as he came closer to her. His dark hair was windblown and damp. "I would expect nothing less from you, Miss Grey."

She tilted her head back to look up into his brutally handsome face.

There was something dark in his gaze. Something indescribably weary. The smoothly ruthless playboy looked strangely troubled in a way she'd never seen before.

Against her will, worry and concern for him smothered her heart as the mist deepened into rain, splattering noisily against the dark trees above.

"Are you…are you all right, Mr. Cruz?"

He stiffened.

"Perfect," he said coldly. He clearly resented her intrusion.

Louisa tightened her hands against the basket handle, furious at herself. What was she thinking? She knew better than to ask a personal question. If her ten months of house management training hadn't taught her that, living for five years as Rafael Cruz's house-keeper in Paris certainly should have!

He never showed his feelings. She'd tried to do the same. It had been easy for the first year or two. Then somehow, in spite of her best efforts, she'd started to care....

Looking at him now, all she could think about was the last time she'd seen his face, the night she'd realized she was hopelessly, wretchedly in love with her playboy boss. She'd been sobbing alone in the kitchen when he'd come home unexpectedly early from a date with yet another impossibly beautiful woman.

"Why are you crying?" he'd asked in a low voice. She'd tried to lie, to tell him she just had something in her eye, but when their eyes had met she'd been unable to speak. Unable to move as he walked directly to her. He'd taken her in his arms and she'd known, down to her bones, that it could only end in her own heartbreak. And yet she couldn't push him away. How could she, when she loved him, this untamable, forbidden man who could never truly be hers?

In his penthouse near the Champs-Élysées, against the backdrop of the sparkling city and the Eiffel Tower lit up like a beacon in the night, he'd exhaled her name in a growl. He'd grabbed her wrists and pushed her against the kitchen wall, kissing her so savagely that all she could do was gasp out his name in the first shock of explosive, mutual need and the joint hunger of their embrace.

She'd wanted him with desire she'd repressed for years. But how could she have ever allowed herself to surrender, knowing it could only end badly?

And that was before she'd even started to worry she might be pregnant…

Don't think about it! she ordered herself desperately. She couldn't be pregnant. If she were, Rafael would never forgive her. He'd think she'd done it on purpose, that she'd lied to him!

She licked her lips. "I'm…glad you're well," she faltered.

His dark slate eyes traced her face, lingering on her mouth before he abruptly turned away, slinging his overnight bag over his shoulder. "Bring dinner to my room," he barked.

He stalked into the house without looking back.

"At once, sir," she whispered as the rain fell faster. Heavy droplets pounded against her face and body, plastering her hair to her head and smearing her glasses.

After her boss disappeared into the mansion, she was able to breathe again. Protecting the basket of roses from the rain with her gray woolen blazer, she fell into step behind the two male assistants carrying his suitcases from the limousine now parked in the carriage house.

The fading ribbons of sunset streaked red across the low clouds as Louisa entered the grand foyer of the nineteenth-century mansion. She carefully wiped her feet before noting her boss's wet footprints across the marble that would now need to be meticulously recleaned. Her eyes followed the dirty footsteps up the sweeping stairs. She saw his dark head and broad-shouldered back disappear behind the landing to his bedroom suite.

The house felt so different now he was here. Rafael Cruz electrified everything. Especially her.

The men followed him up the stairs with the suitcases, and once she was alone, Louisa leaned against the wall, her legs sagging with relief.

Their first meeting was over. It was done.

It seemed that Rafael—*Mr. Cruz,* she corrected herself angrily. His first name kept sneaking into her mind!—had already forgotten all about their night of passion in Paris.

Now if only she could do the same.

Her eyes looked again toward the second-floor landing. But why had he seemed so troubled? Something was very wrong, and she knew it had nothing to do with their one-night stand. Women were interchangeable to him. Easily forgotten. Completely replaceable. No woman could ever touch Rafael's heart.

So if not for a woman, what had brought him to Istanbul three days early—and in such a black mood? She stared up the empty stairs toward his room. She suddenly yearned to know what troubled him. Yearned to offer him solace, some kind of comfort...

No!

She stomped on the thought angrily. Every woman thought Rafael needed comforting.

It was part of his seduction, something he used ruthlessly to his advantage. Women were drawn by his brutish, brooding charm, imagining him a modern Heathcliff with a darkly haunted past. They all yearned to comfort the world-weary Argentinian millionaire with the handsome face and whisper of a broken heart. Louisa had already seen endless women delude themselves into thinking they, and only they, could save his soul. Only Louisa knew the truth.

Rafael Cruz had no soul.

And yet she loved him. She was a fool! Because she, of all women, knew the kind of man he really was—cold, ruthless and unforgiving!

Swear to me you can't get pregnant, Louisa, he'd said to her that breathless night. *I cannot get pregnant,* she'd said.

If it turned out she'd lied to him…

I'm not pregnant, she repeated to herself furiously. *It's impossible!*

And yet, she was afraid to take the test that would tell her for sure. She told herself she was just late. Very late.

Leaving her wet shoes at the front door, she carried the basket of roses into a little mudroom near the large modern kitchen. She filled an expensive crystal vase with water, then arranged the roses carefully inside it. She cleaned the pruning shears and put them away in their drawer. Going up to her room upstairs, she removed her wet clothes, replacing them with a new gray skirt suit as plain and serviceable as the first. She tidied her brown hair back into a severe bun, dried the rain off her glasses with a towel, then gave a single glance at herself in the mirror as she passed. She looked plain and orderly and invisible—just as she wished.

She'd never wanted Rafael to notice her. She'd prayed he wouldn't. After what had happened at her last job, invisibility felt like her only protection. But somehow, it had failed her. Somehow, he'd noticed her anyway. Why had he taken her to his bed? Pity? Convenience?

She took a deep breath, squaring her shoulders. Then she carried the vase of roses into the kitchen.

Almost immediately, her spirits lifted. The kitchen, along with the rest of the mansion, had changed quite a bit in the month since Louisa had arrived here. Her constant attention, working eighteen-hour days to hire staff and oversee cleaning and remodeling of the once-faded house, had turned it into a well-run home. Louisa gently touched the polished wood of the door frame, smiling down at the colorful, gleaming mosaic floor. Overseeing this mansion's restoration to its former glory had been a huge amount of work, but had given her a great deal of pleasure.

Once, it had been neglected. Now it was loved. *Treasured.*

Louisa set her jaw stubbornly. So she wouldn't allow one moment of weakness to force her out of this job she'd loved with such passion for five years. She'd been a convenient woman for Rafael to take to his bed, nothing more. She loved him, but she would try her best to kill that love.

She would do her job. Keep her distance. *Try to forget how he'd taken her virginity.*

She'd forget the way his lips had pressed against hers, so hot and hard and demanding. She'd forget the sensation of his powerful body pressing her to the wall. Forget his strength and the dark hunger in his eyes as he'd lifted her up in his strong arms, and carried her without a word to his bed....

Louisa stood for a moment, alone in the kitchen. Then she started. What had she been doing here? Right. Making his dinner. The cook had gone home sick. She only hoped he had the same hideous stomach flu she'd had in Paris six weeks ago, so he'd be right as rain in three days, in time for Rafael's birthday dinner. She could make simple dishes, but she was no chef. Her cooking skills tended more toward baking cakes and brownies than preparing *chimichurri* sauce for flank steak or preparing a piquant *cazuela de mariscos,* a seafood stew in tomato broth, for a party of twelve!

But like the captain of a ship, she had learned to do nearly every task that running a vast home required. She quickly put together a simple but delicious sandwich using sliced ham and her own freshly homemade bread from the well-stocked pantry. She looked down at the tray and carefully smoothed the linen napkin beneath the silver utensils. She hesitated, then added a small bud vase, in which she placed a newly budding red rose.

There was nothing wrong with adding a rose, she told herself. It was not the act of a lover, but of a housekeeper who cared about details. Nothing had changed. *Nothing.*

She summoned a maid. "Take this tray to Mr. Cruz, please."

The newly hired maid shifted weight from one foot to the other as she picked up the tray. She looked nervous.

With an inward sigh, Louisa patted her on the shoulder encouragingly. "Do not be afraid. Mr. Cruz is…a kind man." She was surprised a lightning bolt didn't strike her dead for that lie. "He will not hurt you." That, at least, was true. He liked his homes and businesses to run smoothly, so he did not ever seduce members of his staff—ever.

At least not until a month ago, when he'd thrown Louisa against his bed and ripped off her clothes. When she'd reached for him so urgently as he fell upon her naked body, and they both were devoured by their hunger and urgent need—

No! *No!*

"Please take it at once," Louisa choked out.

With a nod, the maid took the tray and left the kitchen. But Louisa had barely started washing up the dishes when the girl returned, covered with ham and Dijon mustard smeared down her apron and the rose hanging precariously from her newly wet hair!

"What happened?" Louisa gasped.

The young maid looked close to tears. "He threw the tray at me!" She held the silver tray in one hand and a cracked plate in the other. The accent of her schoolgirl English thickened in her stress. "He says he'll only have you serving him, miss!"

Louisa sucked in her breath.

"He *threw* the *tray?*" Louisa was shocked at the thought of her boss losing control. For heaven's sake, what had happened? Had he lost a business deal? Lost a lot of money? What was wrong with him? For him to be so violent and uncivilized as to actually *throw a tray*—

Louisa's eyes narrowed. Whatever had happened—even if he'd lost the entirety of his fortune—that gave him no excuse to be vicious to a member of her staff! "Give me the tray, Behiye. Then go home."

"Oh, no, miss, please don't sack me—"

"You have just been given the rest of the week off with full pay." She gave a brief smile, covering up her internal rage. "A vacation courtesy of Mr. Cruz, who regrets his brutish behavior very much."

"Thank you, miss."

And if he doesn't regret his behavior yet, Louisa thought furiously as the girl left, *he soon will.*

Louisa's rage built to burning point as she tossed the ceramic plate, once a beautiful specimen of antique Iznik blue-and-white porcelain, into the trash. She washed the silver tray and reassembled the entire meal on a new plate, grimly adding a fresh rose in a silver vase. She made another sandwich, exactly the same as the first, and carried it up the sweeping, curving stairs to the second floor.

She gave a single hard knock on his bedroom door.

"Enter," his voice said harshly.

Still furious, Louisa pushed open the door. Then she stopped.

His bedroom was dark.

"Miss Grey." She heard his low, sardonic voice unseen from the darkness. "So good of you to follow my orders."

His voice was deep, combative. *Hostile.*

Peering into the darkness, Louisa saw him

sitting on a chair in the shadows, in front of the cold fireplace. She set down the tray on a nearby table and, crossing the room in her sensible two-inch heels, she pulled down a switch to turn on the small lamp.

A circle of yellow light illuminated the darkness, revealing a bedroom that was masculine, Spartan and severe.

"Turn that off," he growled, his gaze whirling on her. The blast of angry heat in his gaze nearly caused her to stagger back.

Then, straightening, Louisa clenched her hands into fists. "You won't intimidate me like you did poor Behiye. How dare you attack a maid, Mr. Cruz? *Throwing a tray at her?* Have you quite lost your mind?"

His eyes narrowed as he slowly rose to his feet.

"It is none of your business."

But she stood firm. "Oh, but it is. You pay me to oversee this household. How do you expect me to do that when you terrorize the staff?"

"I did not throw the tray at her," he growled. "I knocked it out of her hand to the floor. She is the one who tried to catch it. Foolishly."

Spoken like a man who'd never cleaned his own floor. "You frightened her!"

His gray eyes gleamed at her in the shadowy light. "An accident," he bit out. "It was...careless of me." Turning away, he set his jaw. "Give the girl the rest of the day off."

She lifted her chin. "You already did, sir. In fact, you just gave her a week's vacation with full pay."

There was a pause in the darkness. "Miss Grey." His voice sounded suddenly odd, almost wistful. "You seem to always know what I need. Sometimes even before I do."

The look he gave her made her heart catch in her throat. As if he needed something very much right now and wished she knew what, without him saying a word.

She felt his look with a flood of heat. Against her will, she was reminded of how it had felt when he'd kissed her... No. She wouldn't think about that night. Couldn't!

"It's my job to know what you'll want," she said evenly, folding her arms. "You pay me to know."

The words *you pay me* hung between them, dividing them.

"Yes," he said in a low voice. "I do."

He turned away, but not before she caught the stark look in his eyes. The same look she'd seen on his face when he'd first come through the garden gate. It wasn't anguish, exactly, but a flash of vulnerability. Of weariness. Loneliness. But that was ridiculous. How could the most ruthless playboy in Europe ever be lonely?

"You never should have sent the maid," he said in a low, dangerous voice. "I told you specifically I wished for *you* to bring me dinner. Not some maid. You."

He wanted to be alone with her?

Exhilaration flooded through her. Then fear overwhelmed everything. She couldn't allow herself to be seduced again, couldn't!

She kept her expression unmoved, hiding her emotions behind layers of her training as she'd been taught. Formality was her strongest weapon. Her only weapon.

"I regret I did not correctly understand your request, sir," she said stiffly. "I have brought up a newly prepared sandwich for your dinner." She gave him a little bow. "Now, if you please, I will leave you to the peace and tranquility of your own company."

"Stop."

Something in his voice made her obey. Slowly she turned back to face him.

His face was dark. He came close to her, almost touching. "I never should have done it."

"Thrown the tray?" she agreed.

His dark eyes seared through hers. "Made love to you in Paris."

For a moment, she couldn't breathe.

Her desire for her boss threatened everything she held dear. Her career. Her self-respect. *Her soul.*

She forced herself to straighten. "I don't remember any such incident, sir."

"Don't you?" he said in a low voice. He reached down to stroke her cheek. His fingertips were featherlight as he turned her chin to meet his gaze, and she shivered at his touch, at the intensity of his dark eyes. "If you cannot remember it, then I must have been mistaken," he whispered. "I didn't kiss you, then. I didn't feel your body trembling against mine."

"No, you didn't." She could hear the rasp of her own breath, was choked by the frantic beating of her heart. "It never happened."

He leaned forward. "Then why," he said, "have I thought of nothing else?"

Her knees shook. She was so close to surrender. So close to acting like all the others, to flinging herself at him. But there could be only one end to that. She'd seen it played out too many times.

Rafael Cruz was ruthless. He broke women's hearts with careless pleasure.

If she let herself want him—he would be the poison that killed her.

She shook her head desperately. "I don't remember you so much as kissing me."

"Perhaps," he said softly, "this will remind you."

Lowering his head, he kissed her.

His lips seared hers, scorching her entire body with that one point of contact. She felt his arms around her, pulling her close, closer still until his large, muscular body seemed to surround her on all sides. She was lost, lost in him. His tongue swept hers, causing every nerve ending from her nipples to her earlobes to her toes to sizzle and contract.

He kissed her, and against her will, she surrendered.

CHAPTER TWO

RAFAEL CRUZ had broken many hearts, and he did not feel particularly bad about it.

He wasn't being arrogant. It was simply a fact.

Every woman he'd ever taken to his bed had objected when he'd inevitably ended the affair. They always wanted more. They turned from flirtatious, seductive, powerful women into clingy shrews sobbing for another chance. No wonder he so rarely slept with a woman more than once or twice. Because once he'd possessed them, the women inevitably changed and lost every quality that had originally attracted him in the first place.

He never lied to any of them. He always told them the truth—that their affair would not last long or be based on anything but physical attraction. If women surrendered their bodies and hearts in a way that ultimately caused them pain, well, that was not his fault. They were adults. They made their own choices. He was not to blame.

But he'd sworn long ago never to seduce an employee. Not out of any concern over a workplace harassment suit—he laughed at that idea—but because the fallout would have made his life inconvenient. And Rafael Cruz must never be inconvenienced.

The world was full of beautiful women to fill his bed. But good employees were hard to find.

Louisa Grey was not merely a competent employee; she was exceptional. She'd become indispensable in his life. She made all his homes run smoothly. After five years, he couldn't imagine his life without her.

She'd never once tried to lure him. Unlike the often clumsy attempts of every woman from his elderly secretary to the cocktail waitress at the bar to gain his notice. Louisa had barely seemed to notice he was a man. *That made him want her most of all.* She was so mysterious. She never spoke of her feelings; never spoke of her past. She had a cool reserve, and hid her beauty beneath glasses and awful clothes.

Still, he'd promised himself he'd never seduce an employee, and he never had once been tempted to break that vow.

Until a month ago.

A mistake. His seduction of Miss Grey had been momentary lapse of willpower. From now on, he had promised himself he would have some self-control.

She was his lead house manager. She coordinated between all his homes around the world. He could not afford to lose her. And women always fell apart when he ended affairs—even previously independent, strong women always turned clingy, whining and desperate in the end. If their night together turned into a full-blown affair, the only end would be the termination of Louisa's employment. Either she would quit, or he would be forced to fire her.

His only hope of keeping her where she belonged—directing his home and satisfying his needs before he was even half-aware of them—was to keep her at a distance.

But his resolve had disappeared from the moment he saw her today.

He'd had a horrible day. Arriving in Istanbul—too late, too late!—his whole body had been knotted up in tension and grief and fury.

Returning from his father's funeral, the father he'd never known, he'd felt so tense his muscles had ached with his rage and failure. His chauffeur had opened the door, and as Rafael had gotten out beneath the drizzling rain, he'd loosened his tie and headed for his house, intending to seek a tall glass of whiskey and perhaps to send his private jet to Paris to collect his latest French flirtation and deliver her to Istanbul. He'd told himself his one-night-stand with his housekeeper had been a mistake that must never be repeated. *It must be forgotten.*

Then he'd seen Louisa in the twilight of the garden behind the mansion. Standing beneath the cypress and fig trees, she'd been holding a basket of freshly cut roses. She looked even more beautiful than he remembered, more sensual and desirable than he could bear. Looking out at the dark waters of the Bosphorus toward Asia, she'd had an expression of wonderment and wistfulness.

Louisa Grey was an oasis of calm and comfort in this chaotic, cold world.

Rafael had promised himself he wouldn't touch her. But when she'd turned to him with her wide, black-fringed eyes, he'd looked at her slender body beneath those shapeless, ugly clothes. He'd known from that moment that he would have her again, no matter what it cost him.

He'd ordered her to come up to his bedroom. Tense and pacing, he'd waited for her. Then he'd been surprised by the maid with the tray. Later, when Louisa had deigned to come up to his room, she'd defied him as no one else dared. She'd tormented him—provoked him. Finally, when she'd drawn up her shoulders and said in a voice full of bravado, *I don't remember you so much as kissing me,* something inside him had snapped.

He'd seized her.

Now, kissing Louisa was heaven. Her lips were so soft and sweet and yielding beneath his. Her skin smelled like soap and spring flowers. His whole body tightened with the force of his desire.

It was more than desire. He knew this was wrong—forbidden—but he longed for her in a way he'd never felt for any woman. The elusive Miss Grey. When he felt her surrender in his arms, a growl rose in the back of his throat. He wrapped his arms around her more tightly and started to pull her back toward the bed.

With a gasp, Louisa wrenched away from him. "No!"

"Louisa—"

"No." She stumbled back from him violently. "We can't do this!"

He reached his arms out for her. "We must."

She jumped back another two steps. With a shuddering intake of breath, she put her fingertips on her lips as if she could still feel him kissing her. "I can't," she whispered. "I work for you."

He knew she was right. That just made him more angry, more determined to have her.

"It doesn't matter," he said fiercely.

"Oh, but it does. You have a rule, Mr. Cruz," she said, lifting her chin. Her beautiful chocolate-colored eyes glittered. "You never seduce your employees. That's the one line you don't cross!"

He craved her desperately. She was the

one tonic that would make him forget everything he'd lost today. But he could not tell her that. He must never appear vulnerable to anyone—not to any woman on earth, let alone one of his employees!

"It is my rule, not yours," he said coolly. "I can choose to make an exception."

But she stepped back, out of his reach.

"I choose differently," she said. "What happened between us in Paris was a mistake. It will never happen again. I can't lose my career, my reputation, my life," she whispered. "Not again!"

He frowned, trying to read her expression.

"What do you mean, *again?*"

She blinked fast as she looked away. "Nothing."

"I don't believe you." He knew little about her past beyond what was spelled out on her résumé. She'd always deflected personal questions with cool, dignified reserve.

She turned to him sharply. "Paris," she muttered. "I meant Paris."

"You didn't mean Paris."

"What else?"

Another deflection. He narrowed his eyes.

"There was another man before me," he guessed.

"You know there wasn't!"

"You were a virgin. That doesn't mean there wasn't another man." The thought made his shoulders feel tighter still.

She set her jaw stubbornly. "You checked my references. You know all about me."

Rafael didn't know half what he wished he knew. He'd been so impressed by her at the interview that he'd done only the barest measure of due diligence above and beyond what the exclusive employment agency had provided. He never liked to rely totally on underlings. He'd spoken to the wife of her last employer, and the woman had raved up and down the moon about Louisa Grey, calling her "amazing" and a "treasure." It seemed very unlikely that she would have spoken so highly about Louisa if she'd suspected her husband of having an affair with her.

It didn't make sense.

"What are you hiding?" Rafael said, his eyes searching her face. "You never mention family or friends back home. Why? Why do you never want to go home?"

He saw her eyes widen, heard her intake

of breath. Then she smoothed her oversize gray woolen skirt beneath her trembling hands. "It doesn't matter." She turned away. "If there will be nothing else, sir, I will leave you now—"

"No, damn it." He crossed the room in two steps, blocking the doorway so she could not leave. "I won't let you go. Not until you answer me. I…" *I need you,* he almost said, but the words caught in his throat as sharply as a razorblade. He hadn't said them to anyone for years. He'd created his whole life to avoid saying them.

Through the open window, he could see the lights of Istanbul flickering in the dusk. Black silhouettes of minarets plunged like daggers into the dying red sunset. He could hear a muezzin's broadcasted call to prayers echo across the sea.

His eyes locked with hers in the shadowy room. The tension between them changed. Electrified. Desire for her swept through him, negating all else.

"Get out of my way, Mr. Cruz," she whispered.

He could hear the quickness of her breath, see the rise and fall of her chest. "No."

"You can't keep me here!"

Rafael almost shook with the force of his need for her.

"Can't I?" he said softly.

He wanted to bury himself in her so deeply that he would forget everything—everything that threatened to break him apart. He heard the quick pant of her breath. He took a deep breath of her, smelling her fragrance, soap and clean cotton and freshly cut roses.

If he were smart, he would let her go. He would find a different woman to fill his bed. The pouting French starlet he'd been flirting with for the last few days. Her. Anyone.

Anyone but Louisa Grey.

His eyes fell to her mouth. Her beautiful bow-shaped lips were pink and bare of makeup. Something about Louisa intrigued him beyond his understanding. He wanted her in a way that almost felt against his will. He craved the mind-numbing pleasure he'd felt making love to her. The best sex of his life.

The pleasure of her body would help him forget his pain. She would be the drug to distract him from his grief and despair. He would ravish her in his bed, hard and fast, until the fire in his blood was sated. Until the pain in his heart was obliterated into ash. Then, and only then, would he let her go....

Rafael looked at her from beneath heavily lidded eyes. He saw the tremble of her body in the shadows.

She wanted to escape him—to deny them both what they both wanted.

But this inexperienced girl was no match for his will. She'd been a virgin when he'd first taken her in Paris. She would not be able to resist him now. He would possess her until he was utterly satiated, until he felt her writhe and shake beneath his body.

Slowly, implacably, Rafael pulled her into his arms.

She tried to resist, but he would not let her go. She trembled, tilting her head back to look up into his face. Tall as she was for a woman, he still towered over her. Her beautiful brown eyes glistened in the faint golden light.

"Please," she said in a low voice. "Let me go."

His hands tightened on her. "Are you so afraid?" he said quietly.

She drew a shuddering breath. "Yes."

He cupped her face. "Of me?"

"No," she said in a low voice. "If you kiss me again, if you take me to your bed, I'm afraid…"

"Afraid of what?"

She blinked fast, her full lashes black against her pale skin.

"Afraid I'll die of wanting you," she whispered.

He nearly gasped.

Reaching up, Louisa put her hand on his rough cheek. "I've missed you," she said in a voice full of anguish. "I've missed you so…."

He shook beneath her touch. Taking her hand in his own, he fervently kissed the palm, then pulled her into his arms. Lowering his mouth to hers, he kissed her. Deeply. Hungrily.

He kissed her with all the repressed desire of the month they'd been apart—and of all the wasted years before that.

Louisa trembled.

Rafael's touch burned her. It frightened her. *Seduced her.*

He kissed her, his powerful lips moving

over hers. Guiding her. Giving her such explosive pleasure, causing electricity to sizzle down her limbs beneath her gray woolen suit until she thought she might die of this ache like fire.

Too many years of repressed desire could no longer be contained. It was all she could do not to blurt out the two devastating secrets that would destroy everything.

She was completely, irrevocably in love with a man who never wanted to be either husband or father. And she might be pregnant with his child….

Rafael's hand on the back of her head, stroking through her hair and the bare skin of her neck, created a spark that seared up and down her body. Her breasts became heavy, her nipples tight. She tingled with painful awareness all over her body. She wanted him so much it drove her to despair.

"Forget I'm your boss," he murmured against her skin. She felt the warmth of his breath, the roughness of his jawline against her cheek. "Stay with me tonight."

She was overwhelmed by the sensuality of his hands on her body, his fingers stroking her back down to her hips.

He pulled back from her and golden light flickered in his dark eyes like the hot flames in hell. "Stay with me," he commanded.

Her gaze fell to his lips. She could barely breathe. She wanted to say yes. Wanted it so badly she thought she'd die. But...

"I can't," she gasped, even as her fingers tightened on his black shirt. She licked her lips. "If the rest of the staff ever found out I'd been your mistress...they'd lose all respect for me."

"It's no business of theirs—"

"I'd lose all respect for myself!"

For answer, he touched her hair. Pulling out the pins that held her hair in a tight bun, he let it tumble down her shoulders. "So beautiful," he whispered, moving his fingers through the long chestnut waves. He looked into her eyes. "Why don't you ever let it down?"

Her hair? Or her guard?

His fingers felt so deliciously light moving through her hair. She held her breath. Her scalp tingled as he stroked whisper-light touches against her earlobes and neck then cradled the back of her head in both of his hands. He looked down at her.

"You work miracles." He looked around the newly remodeled bedroom with wonder. "No one could ever feel anything for you... but respect."

She exhaled. His words were balm to her.

But she knew how the world truly worked. Her spine snapped straight.

"Reputations are destroyed by affairs like this. No one would ever hire me for a respectable job again."

"Why would you ever leave me?" He lifted a dark eyebrow. "No woman ever wants to leave."

He spoke the words as a joke, but Louisa knew they were true. She also knew that she couldn't possibly remain his housekeeper as his discarded mistress. That she'd already given him her body once was bad enough—it had forced her to flee to Istanbul.

She was still able to work for him, barely. But she did have some pride. If she gave herself to him completely, if she admitted that she was in love with him, she knew she'd never recover from his scorn. She'd never survive loving him, working for him—and seeing him move on to another woman.

Especially if she was pregnant…

I'm not pregnant, she repeated to herself, but the words had become hollow and metallic. She gritted her teeth. All right, fine. She would take the test. *Tonight.* As soon as she was alone. Then she would know for sure that she had nothing to fear. Or else she'd have some shocking news for Rafael Cruz—the heartless, ruthless, charming playboy—and she'd have to tell him she was going to make him a father against his will.

He would never forgive her. He would never believe something had gone wrong with the Pill, that her cycle must have been thrown off by those two days of bad flu she'd had a week or two before their affair. She'd given him her word of honor she couldn't get pregnant. He'd be furious. He'd think she'd lied.

Or worse: that she'd gotten pregnant on purpose to trap him. Louisa had overheard more than one of his cast-off mistresses plotting cold-bloodedly to get pregnant in a stupid, selfish attempt to marry him. He'd evaded their plots easily. So how would he feel being unintentionally trapped by his own housekeeper?

"You're shivering," Rafael murmured. He pulled her closer into his arms. "Are you cold?"

Unable to answer, she shook her head.

He stroked her cheek.

"Let me warm you," he whispered.

His head lowered toward hers.

"No!" She pushed away from Rafael with strength she hadn't known she had. From across the room, they stared at each other, not touching, in the shadows. The only sound was the ragged pant of her breath. She turned away.

"I need you, Louisa," he said behind her. "Don't go."

Not turning around, she closed her eyes. "You don't need me," she replied hoarsely. "There are women aplenty to fill your bed. You have your pick of them. You don't need me."

"I found him," she heard Rafael say behind her. "My father."

She froze in the doorway. With a gasp, she whirled around.

Across the large bedroom, Rafael stood like a statue chiseled in ice. His handsome face was stark and strange, half-illuminated by the window's slanted beam of moonlight.

"You found your father?" she choked out, clasping her hands. "Oh, Rafael, I'm so glad! You've been looking for him for so long!"

"Yes."

His voice was harsh and jagged as a rusty knife. Louisa frowned at him in bewilderment. Why did he not look pleased? Why did he still look so frozen and strange?

Rafael had been looking for his father for twenty years, ever since the Argentinian man who'd raised him had revealed on his deathbed that Rafael wasn't truly his son. His stepfather had told him before he'd died that, the week before he'd married her, Rafael's mother had returned from Istanbul—pregnant.

"Is your father here?" Louisa breathed. "In Istanbul? Have you talked to him?"

"His name was Uzay Çelik," Rafael cut her off. He looked toward the window. "And he died two days ago."

"Oh, no," she whispered, her heart in her throat. Against her will, she walked back across the bedroom toward him as he stared into the flickering lights across the dark waters of the Bosphorus. "Your investigators found him too late."

Slowly he turned to her.

"They never found him at all. My mother is the one who finally told me. After twenty years of silence, she overnighted a letter to Paris that I received this morning. After he was dead."

The hurt in his voice, the pain like a boy's, caught at her throat. And Louisa could hold herself back no longer. Reaching out, she placed her hand on his back, rubbing his tight muscles and his strong, powerful, hunched shoulders. "Why did she wait so long to tell you?"

He gave a harsh laugh. "To hurt me, I suppose," he said. "She doesn't know that it's impossible. I'll never be hurt again—not by her or anyone."

The bleakness of his tone belied his words.

"But surely," Louisa persisted, "your mother loves you—"

His lip curled. "She sent me a letter and a package that arrived in Paris today." He held up a gold signet ring. "She'd saved it for thirty-seven years, since before I was born.

Now she sends it to me. Now, when it's too late."

Louisa's heart turned over in her chest at the pain in his handsome face. She knew what finding his real father had meant to Rafael.

"I barely made it to the funeral. There were only five mourners, and they seemed to have shown up with the thought of asking surviving family members for money. Debts are all my father left behind. No wife. No other children. No friends. Just debts."

"I'm so sorry," Louisa whispered, desperate to take the pain out of his eyes, feeling helpless. "I'll contact your guests and tell them the birthday dinner is canceled."

His gaze became hard. "Why?"

"Because, because," she stammered, "you're in mourning."

He shook his head. "The dinner party will go on as planned."

"Are you sure? You don't have to do this."

He didn't answer. Instead he looked around the beautiful room. He gave a low laugh. "I bought this palace for my father, for when I found him. Now all I have left—" his hand tightened into a fist around the gold ring hanging on a chain "—is this."

She pressed her hand against his rough cheek, looking up into his face. "If only there was something I could do, if only—"

"There is."

And he kissed her.

His lips were fierce, demanding. She could not stop him or pull away; all she could do was surrender to his strength, and the force of her own desire.

His hands moved over her clothes in the soft circle of pale golden light amid the shadows. He stroked her arms, her belly. Pulling off her woolen blazer and dropping it gently to the floor, he cupped her breasts through her thin cotton shirt. She gasped. Then, with a soft moan, she wrapped her arms around his neck and pulled him closer.

He pushed her back against the bed, still kissing her. He moved with increasing urgency, pulling up her blouse, reaching beneath her silk bra to caress her breasts. Her nipples hardened to small pebbles beneath his muscular fingers as she held him close, aching for his touch. But it wasn't enough… wasn't nearly enough!

With sudden impatience, he pulled open the blouse in a single swift movement, popping the buttons. He ripped her flimsy silk bra in half easily, pushing the cups apart and lowering his head to suckle her.

She gasped, arching beneath his mouth. As he licked and bit one nipple, his powerful hand squeezed the other breast, sending sparks of longing down her body, between her legs.

Lifting his head, cupping both her breasts in his large hands, he gave her a hard, possessive kiss that bruised her lips. But amid the pain was an intensity of pleasure, the need of her own longing that drove her almost insane.

She had to stop this.

She would die if she stopped this.

As he kissed her, she felt the weight of his body, fully clothed and so much larger than her own, pressing her heavily into the firm mattress. His mouth plundered hers, his tongue tantalizing and mastering her. She felt his powerful hands move down her body. Grabbing her skirt's hemline at the knee, he pulled it up until her legs were bare all the way to her hips.

He continued to kiss her fiercely, holding her body to the bed with his weight. One hand moved between her legs, caressing between her naked thighs. She sucked in her breath. She tried to move, to push him away from her, but she could not. Her mind was no longer in control of her body. Her body wanted what it wanted—*and it wanted him.*

His hand cupped between her legs, and she gasped. He cut off her gasp with a hard kiss, stealing her protest away, leaving her beyond the ability to fight what they both wanted. He moved his hand beneath her white cotton panties, caressing her slick folds like molten heat with a thick finger, caressing her sensitive core with his thumb.

She gasped, arching off the bed.

He pulled away, looking down at her. His eyes were dark.

Then he yanked her panties off her body in a swift movement, tossing them to the floor. Before reason could start to return, before she could remember she should tell him *No, please, we must stop,* he knelt before her on the bed. Pushing her legs apart, he moved his head between her legs and took a long, languorous taste.

She gave a high-pitched cry, gripping the pillow beneath her head with both hands.

Holding her hips firmly, refusing to allow her to move away, he held her to him. He licked her, lapping her one moment and suckling her the next. His tongue flicked inside her. Then fingers followed, with rough sensuality she could not deny or escape.

With all his experience, he knew just what to do. He played her like an instrument. He knew how to make her sing. The pleasure was so intense she nearly wept.

She felt the first waves of aching fulfillment start to crest, building inside her. Just as her hips started to lift of their own volition against his mouth, just as her whole body started to tremble and shake, he released her. As she cried out in frustration, he rose to his feet. He pulled down his pants. He did not wait to remove the rest of his clothes before climbing on top of her and covering her body with his own. She felt his hardness seeking entry between her legs for one brief second and he brutally thrust himself inside her. A sharp explosion of agonizing pleasure ripped through her as she felt him impale her so deeply. Pinning her with his massive size and weight, he thrust again, more deeply still and her whole body hummed, tense as a bow. The sweet agony coiled inside her, climbing higher…then still higher…until she could not breathe, until she thought she could bear no more, until she thought she would break.

He pulled back and rode her, holding her hips with his big hands to penetrate her so deep and wide and hard she felt split in two. She moaned, holding her hands against the black headboard, writhing from side to side as he shoved inside her again and again. She had to bite her lip to keep herself from moaning his name, from begging him to not stop, from begging him to love her and never leave…

With a growl, he pushed one last time inside her so deep it shattered her apart into a thousand glimmering pieces. He nearly pierced her heart, and as her world exploded, from a distance she heard herself scream his name.

* * *

The next morning, Rafael woke up to find his lead housekeeper, the most prized member of his staff, naked and sleeping beside him in bed.

He nearly groaned aloud. He'd done it. *Again.* After promising himself he'd never touch Louisa again!

Sunlight was shining bright through the tall windows of his bedroom. The dark wood and new furniture, with shining steel fixtures and stark glass lights, had an oddly warm appearance beneath the soft golden light pouring from the windows. Or maybe the golden glow came from the woman now sleeping beside him. She made everything beautiful.

He looked at her lovely face, surrounded by brown hair tumbling over the pillow in waves. A tender smile still curved her pink lips. Sleeping and naked, she looked so vulnerable. So young.

He cursed himself in low, guttural Spanish.

He'd thought he had some self-control. He'd done everything to try to forget his night with Louisa Grey, and the fact that it had been the single most amazing sexual ex-

perience of his life. Which with all his experience, was incredible.

Perhaps that was why he'd been unable to
forget. Uninterested in other women. Unable
to think of anything else.

He still didn't know why she'd been crying
that night in Paris. He'd been shocked when
he'd returned from another dull date to find
Louisa overcome with emotion. Louisa, who
never showed her feelings. He hadn't known
how to deal with it, so he'd taken her in his
arms. And then he'd done what he'd longed
to do for months. He'd kissed her. He'd done
more than kiss her. He'd made passionate,
reckless love to her—and discovered to his
shock that his beautiful, self-contained housekeeper was, at twenty-eight, still a virgin.

Even now, when by all rights he should
have been well satisfied, his body tightened
at the memory of making love to her in Paris.
Of making love to her last night. He felt the
heat off her skin as she lay sleeping beside
him, naked in his bed, and he wanted her
anew.

He looked at her in the morning light. She
looked so beautiful. So impossibly young. So
lush and desirable.

He'd tried to rid himself of his inconvenient desire for her. He'd allowed her to transfer to his Istanbul house, though he did not want her to leave. He'd busied himself with work in Paris. He'd tried to move on with another woman, specifically Dominique Lepetit, though the truth was that the amoral actress was no longer of any interest to him.

Louisa, however...

With a low groan, he rolled over in bed and sat up, holding his head in his hands. He could still not quite believe he'd slept with her without a condom again, something he'd never done with any other woman. Oh, other women had told him they were on the Pill, but he'd never trusted them completely. In the past, he'd either been well-prepared with condoms, or he'd walked away from the situation. Simple as that. He never wanted to have a wife or child or be pinned down in any way. He took freedom even more seriously than he took pleasure.

Rafael glanced back over his shoulder at Louisa, who was still sleeping peacefully, like a child. He immediately felt comforted. Louisa Grey would never lie. If she'd said she was on the Pill, then she was.

He trusted her. In fact, she was the only woman he trusted. She'd been a virgin the first time he'd taken her, for God's sake. That had been an amazing discovery during an incredible night. And last night had been even better....

He had the sudden memory of her naked body beneath his, the way she'd felt when he'd pushed inside her. The image of her ecstatic face as he'd possessed her as their sweaty bodies pressed together urgently in the heat of the night.

He'd thought the first time he'd taken her, in Paris, had been the best night he'd ever had with any woman. But last night had been even better. Something about the feel of her skin—or the smell of her hair. Perhaps it was the way she moved, the combination of sensuality mixed with innocence. Or her elusiveness. She always held something of herself back. Always.

Except in his bed.

Whatever the cause, some chemical re-action took hold of his brain whenever he was near her. He, who'd slept with so many women, who had his choice of heiresses and princesses and models, could not stop wanting his housekeeper. Louisa was like a drug to him.

Because she was forbidden?

His smile fell. And he cursed himself anew.

Rising to his feet, he put on a robe and left the well-kept bedroom. He went out to the veranda. He looked down at the garden and the Bosphorus beyond. In a short time, she'd turned this neglected mansion into an exquisite home.

His hands gripped the wrought-iron balcony railing. And now, because of his lust, he would lose her—his most prized employee!

He glanced back at the beautiful woman sleeping in his bed. He had to find a way to return to a simple relationship of boss and employee. But he wasn't sure he could.

From the moment he'd first interviewed her in Paris for the head housekeeper position, he'd been intrigued by her—this pretty young woman who went to some lengths to appear plain, wearing black cat's-eye glasses and oversize, unflattering clothes, pulling her chestnut hair back into a tight bun from which no tendril could hope to escape. She'd left her first position in the household of a financier in Miami, at a very good rate of pay, because apparently she wished to see Europe.

"You will be allowed no vacations," he'd told her at that first interview. "I need a house manager who will have no other desires other than to smoothly and perfectly run my home."

He'd waited for Miss Louisa Grey, a modern young woman, to tell him he was out of his mind with such expectations and to leave his office; instead, she'd just looked up at him with her cool brown eyes.

"Of course."

"I don't think you understand," he'd said evenly. "You won't be able to leave. Not for vacations. Not for Christmas. And do not think I will eventually transfer you to New York. I like stability in my home life. If you start in Paris you will stay here."

"Fine," she'd repeated, frowning up at him with her brow furrowed.

"Fine?" he barked.

"I do not need to go back home."

He'd lifted his eyebrows in disbelief. "Never?"

"Correct. For…for reasons of my own

which I do not care to explain." She lifted her chin. "I will do excellent work for you, Mr. Cruz."

And she had.

Efficient, dedicated Miss Grey had never taken a day off. Never asked for a vacation. Never complained. She'd never asked for a transfer.

Until he'd seduced her.

For the first few years she'd been his housekeeper, she'd acted as if she could barely distinguish Rafael from an intemperate child to be tolerated and tended. Gradually he'd taken it as a challenge. He'd coaxed her out of her shell in the evenings, as he'd eaten a late supper in the kitchen. He'd gradually lured Louisa's warm heart out from beneath her dignified reserve. It had been an amusement. Even—a friendship.

Until he'd seduced her.

He cursed himself again under his breath.

She wasn't just his valued housekeeper, she was the extremely competent manager who coordinated between all his homes in New York, St. Barts, Buenos Aires, Istanbul and Tokyo.

And this would be the end of it. *Qué fastidio!* Now that he'd slept with her twice, it would end badly—as it always did. She would cease to be sensible, useful Miss Grey and become a woman without a shred of reason in her head. She'd be clingy to her fingertips.

Or would she?

Louisa Grey, clingy? The thought was almost laughable. She was so different from all other women. Was it possible, then, that their affair could be different as well?

He still wanted her. Was it possible she could be that legendary creature—a reasonable woman—and they could continue their affair until he was satisfied? Could they enjoy the passion of a love affair—then simply return to their regular lives that were already so convenient and perfect, as employer and employee?

He ached for her as he did for no other woman. A few days and he'd certainly be done with her. That's how all of his affairs ended. If he could just enjoy her in his bed for just a few more days....

"Good morning," he heard her say behind him.

He turned to face her and sucked in his breath.

Louisa stood on the veranda wearing his white oversize robe. The pink sunrise dawning over the minarets of the east brought such beauty to her face. Her smile was quiet and resolute.

He'd never seen anyone more beautiful, with so much sweetness and dignity. She was the most intriguing woman he'd ever met. No woman came close, he realized. Even now, remembering how he'd taken her the night before, he was throbbing with need for her. He wanted to lift her up in his arms, drag her back into his bedroom and throw her on the bed. He wanted to take her again and again, fast and hard, until he'd had his fill.

"Come away with me," he said abruptly.

She laughed playfully, looking around the Ottoman mansion and the incredible view of the Bosphorus. "To get away from all this?"

He frowned, trying to think. He had a hard time thinking straight when she was smiling like that. He remembered suddenly an offer made by an acquaintance selling him real estate in Paris. Xerxes Novros was a cold-hearted bastard but the man had offered the use of his island. "Greece?" he suggested.

She saw he was serious and blinked. Then she shook her head. "Your dinner party is in two days."

"Knowing you, the arrangements are already completed."

She took a deep breath. "But still…"

"I am done with Istanbul," he said harshly. "After the party, I intend to put this house up for sale. I am done here." His dark eyes looked down into hers. "But not done with you."

"I should go." Her voice was small. Unhappy.

"Go?"

"Work for someone else."

He stared at her, dumbfounded. Then his eyebrows lowered. "You can't," he said in a low voice. "I need you."

"What you mean to say is that you like having me work for you. That you find it *convenient*."

"Yes," he said gruffly. "I do. And it is. I see no reason why that should stop."

She gave a low, bitter laugh. "No. Why would you?"

He placed his hands persuasively on her shoulders. "*Mira!* So we've fallen into bed. I've been through this many times. A few days together, and we'll come back and no longer feel this way. Our lives can return to normal. I promise you."

She looked at him, her brown eyes so deep and tender, and for a moment he thought he convinced her. Then she shook her head. "Sure, that is how it works. *For you.* Your mistresses have nervous breakdowns."

"Not you. You would never be like that, Louisa," he said. "You have far too much dignity. Too much sense. That's what I love most about you." He gave her a sudden wicked grin. "Along with your luscious body."

She stared at him for a moment. Then she turned her head, staring off at the Bosphorus, flooded with the brilliant pink light of sunrise.

He took her hands in his own, looking down at her.

"Forget I'm your boss. Forget that you work for me. Take two days and go away with me. Let me pamper you in luxury where no one else knows you. Let someone else serve *you* for a change. Let me give you pleasure," he whispered, stroking the bare skin of her inner wrist, "such as you've never known."

He kissed her lips before she could answer. When he finally pulled away, he whispered into her ear, "Give in. You know I'm going to take you, Louisa. You know you won't be able to resist me. You will be mine."

You will be mine.

Louisa couldn't breathe, she wanted him so much.

She looked into his handsome, ruthless dark gaze and knew she should tell him off—tell him in her devastatingly formal way that she was his housekeeper, nothing more, and she existed to keep his homes organized and well-staffed. To tell him that she had no feelings for him whatsoever as anything more than her boss. But when she looked into the darkness of his eyes, she could not lie.

His touch felt like fire to her.

"All right," she said in a soft voice she almost couldn't recognize as her own.

He pulled back, his fierce eyes searching hers. "Yes?"

"I'll come away with you," she whispered.

He kissed her fervently on the palm, then the back of her hand. A shiver of longing went through her, a shiver that shook her to the core.

She couldn't deny them what they both wanted.

No matter what it cost. She would have two days—two days to be his mistress and know how it felt to be his adored lover. Two days to live on for the rest of her life, when she would love him from a distance, with a broken heart, knowing he would never love her in return.

She only prayed he was right, and that two days of pleasure would cure her of this desperate, hopeless love. She prayed it would satiate her, ending all her longing for Rafael, so she could once again enjoy the job she loved, supervising the housecleaning, managing the staff and arranging his life.

Would she really be able to watch him move on to the next woman and feel nothing? Apparently Rafael thought so. And he knew so much more about love affairs than she. She prayed he was right, and when she returned to Istanbul, she would no longer want him, that she'd no longer love him.

She would be able to take back her heart. She would no longer cry out for him in the cold loneliness of night. This two-day affair could save her.

Unless she was pregnant. Then…it was already too late.

CHAPTER THREE

"Another iced tea, Miss Grey?"

Shading her eyes from the hot Greek sun, Louisa looked up from where she was stretched out on the poolside lounge chair. "Yes," she said, blushing. Being served, rather than the server, still shocked her. "That would be lovely. Thank you."

The Greek servant, who was young and very handsome, handed her the cool drink in a tall glass with a flourish and a respectful, admiring bow before he departed back inside the white walls of the sprawling hillside mansion.

Sipping her drink—which was, incidentally, her third one that afternoon—Louisa stared around her for a moment with shock. She'd been on this private Greek island since yesterday morning, but she still couldn't quite believe that she was the one relaxing, instead of the one rushing around like a madwoman trying to satisfy her employer's wishes. Instead of cleaning and organizing, she was lazily sunning herself in a bikini as her handsome lover did laps in the infinity pool overlooking the blue Aegean Sea.

Taking another sip of her tea, Louisa set it down on the table with a happy sigh. Lifting her arms over her head in a yawn, she glanced at the white mansion behind her. It was huge and luxurious, clinging to the rocky hillside above the sea. She leaned her head back against the lounge chair cushion. The sky was a cloudless, limpid blue. Reaching for her sunglasses, she put them on and picked up her paperback novel. Holding the book over her head to block out the sun, she tried to focus on the page.

She was distracted when she saw Rafael rise from the water. As he climbed out of the pool, she couldn't look away. His tanned skin glistened in the sun as rivulets of water poured down the hard muscles of his body, down the dark hair of his chest, disappearing beneath the small swim trunks slung low across his slim hips.

Her lips suddenly went dry.

"Are you bored, *querida?*" Rafael said huskily, looking at her across the pool deck.

"Yes, very," she managed to tease him.

"Put down that book." He walked slowly across the white stamped concrete floor. Like a lion stalking a gazelle, he never looked away from her. "If you need distraction, I will entertain you."

"I like to read—" she protested weakly, but she could not resist as, for the third time since they'd arrived on this island, he took the book away from her. She had bought the book, a deliciously trashy novel, with high anticipation. But she had yet to finish the first paragraph. Perhaps because her life had taken a sudden turn and was full of more luxury and passion than she could have ever imagined in any fantasy.

Rafael pulled the sunglasses off her face and set them down on the table. He placed both hands on the soft white cushion around her. For a moment, he looked down at her and she was overwhelmed by anticipation, by the scent of him, by the cool feel of his wet skin against her warm body.

Then he lowered his mouth to hers.

She closed her eyes with a sigh of pleasure as he kissed her, searing her bruised lips with the magnetic force of his own. She felt his bare skin against her body, the rough dark hair of his chest pressing against her warm, naked belly. They'd already made love at least a dozen times since they'd arrived here yesterday morning, at this beautiful private island compound borrowed from one of Rafael's wealthy tycoon friends whom she'd never met. Two days of pleasure, of being served cocktails and hors d'oeuvres, of being waited on hand and foot. Two days of nothing but admiration and adoration.

Was this what it felt like to every woman, to be a rich man's mistress?

Or was it just because the man was Rafael, and she blossomed beneath the miracle of his full, devoted attention?

Whatever the reason, Louisa had never felt so beautiful or so desired. She'd never felt so happy. She felt like a different woman. Everyone here treated her as if she were some gorgeous young creature who deserved to be spoiled, her every whim catered to. They treated her as if luxury and admiration were her birthright, and they did it in such a convincing way that she almost was starting to believe it herself. Especially when Rafael kissed her like this...

He pulled away abruptly. His gray eyes were the color of slate, dark with need.

"You look beautiful in this bikini," he growled. "You'd look even better without it."

She looked up at him. Bright sunlight traced the sharp edges of his cheekbones and jawline with shadow. He was so impossibly handsome. So impossible to resist. And here, in this fantastic place, she had no reason to resist him. She wasn't a housekeeper here.

She was Rafael's mistress.

"I'm glad you like the bikini, since you're the one who insisted on buying it—along with the other four." She gave a sudden laugh. "Honestly, Rafael, how many swimsuits do you think a girl needs for a two-day vacation?"

He put his hand on the naked skin between her breasts, barely covered with small triangles of fabric. "If you're the girl, I'd prefer none."

He slowly undid the tie of her bikini.

Pulling it off her body, he dropped the top to the floor.

She tried to cover herself with her hands. "The staff," she whispered.

He stopped her, pulling her hands away.

"They will see nothing," he said between kisses. "They are paid not to see."

He cupped her breasts, then suckled each nipple beneath the bright Greek sun. Slowly he licked his way down her belly before he lazily untied the strings of her bikini bottom. The reflection of the sunlight from the pool dazzled her, causing sparkles like diamonds in her vision. Or maybe it was just the way Rafael touched her….

She closed her eyes. She felt him stroking her, as if she were a precious treasure. *His desired, adored mistress.* He kissed and licked down the length of her tanned belly, his skin now warm against hers. She heard him move, heard his swim trunks fall to the floor, and then he was on top of her….

For just a moment. Her world turned upside down and she opened her eyes in surprise, realizing that he was now beneath her on the lounge chair, and he'd placed her astride him. His hard erection was jutting between her naked legs.

Rafael met her eyes steadily.

She took a deep breath. Then, with some trepidation, she touched him, stroking his shaft gently. He moved beneath her fingers, expanding somehow to even greater size in her hand until she wondered how it was possible he would ever fit again inside her.

"Kiss me," he commanded. She wondered for an instant exactly where he meant her to kiss him, then she felt him drag her shoulders up so he could plunder her mouth with his own. Below, she felt his hardness move against her soft belly, then between her legs, seeking entrance. He kissed her deeply, entwining his tongue with her own, and she involuntarily swayed her hips against him. She felt him jump beneath her, rock hard and huge. Her breasts felt heavy against his dark-haired chest, her nipples tightening to painful intensity as she swayed. The hot Greek sun beat into the naked skin of her back, against the warmth of his smooth skin.

She ached for him. *Ached.* But he wouldn't take her. Though she could see how greatly he desired her, he seemed to be waiting, to be taunting her and luring her to be the one to initiate. He wanted her to be the one to take him.

With an intake of breath, she lowered herself over him, taking him a single inch inside her.

She heard him gasp—or had the sound come from her own lips?

She moved and swayed against him, wrapping tighter and lower in a circular motion, moving the tight molten core of her liquid need against his taut muscular body. With each circle, she moved lower, bringing his shaft deeper and deeper still inside her. She felt him tremble and gasp with his own need but he did not try to force the rhythm or roll her beneath him. He let her control the pace, and when she looked into his face, she could see what that cost him, how close and grimly he was hanging to the ragged edge of his desire.

She finally took him all the way inside her, all the way to the hilt, and for a moment she could not move. She closed her eyes, savoring the feel of him inside her, wishing she could make the moment last forever.

Then she heard the hoarse gasp of his

breath and knew how she was torturing him. She smiled. She moved against him, riding him slow and deep, and the first shuddering wave almost immediately hit her. She gripped his shoulders and held on for dear life as her hips rode him harder and faster. She felt him shudder and shake and he cried out her name. Hearing his name on her lips, her own world exploded, blinding her with a million shards of light and darkness, of white sun and blue sea.

She exhaled.

When she came back to herself, she was lying on top of him. In wonder and amazement, she stared down at her pale hand splayed across his dark-haired chest. Though she'd been sunning herself all day, her skin was still pale and fair compared to his darkly tanned olive hue. Both his strong arms were still wrapped possessively around her body, holding her against him. Rafael's eyes were closed as he slept, a smile of amazed joy still tracing his sensual mouth.

She loved him.

Staring at him, she could not deny it. Deny it? She gloried in it.

She loved him.

Then as she stared at his beautiful face, her smile faded.

She still hadn't taken the test.

With an intake of breath, she lowered her head back against his bare chest, closing her eyes. She hadn't had a single moment alone, and there wasn't exactly a twenty-four-hour drugstore on this island. There was nothing here except the sprawling mansion...and tennis courts...and two pools...and stables... and a vineyard. This entire island was nothing but a rich man's fantasy.

Tomorrow, they would return to Istanbul. She would cease being Rafael's cosseted mistress, and return to being his plain, efficient housekeeper. She would serve the guests at his dinner party, then begin preparations to assist the real estate agent in the sale of the house Louisa had created with such love. *That she'd created for him.*

With her cheek pressed against the rough dark hair of his muscular chest, she stared out blindly at the shimmering blue sea beneath the swimming pool. She'd just started to feel at home in Istanbul. But now, just like Paris—just like Miami—the rug was being pulled out from beneath her.

When would she finally have a home of her own, a home no one could ever take from her?

Louisa blinked fast, staring out at the bright blue sea blending into eternity with the endless blue sky. Memories raced through her, memories she'd tried to avoid for five years. Memories of Matthias…and Katie. *I'm sorry, Louisa. I never meant to get pregnant.*

Would she ever have enough distance in space and time that her past would no longer haunt her?

She felt Rafael's hand brush against her cheek. She looked up at him.

"What is it, Louisa?" he said softly. His gray eyes seared her, searching her soul. "What are you thinking about?"

With an intake of breath, she looked away. She hadn't told him about her past. She hadn't spoken of it to anyone.

Five years ago, she'd been stabbed to the heart by the two people she loved most in the world. She'd fled the United States for a fresh start. She'd changed her bright, formfitting clothes to plain, serviceable gray ones, boxy, shapeless suits. She'd lost her appetite. She'd lost weight. She'd started wearing glasses instead of contacts and pulled her brown hair back in a tight bun. She'd done everything she could do to make sure no man would ever notice her again.

She found a new job in Paris. She hadn't feared to work for Rafael. She knew she would be safe from any playboy's charms. She'd worked constantly, literally lived at her workplace, and hadn't taken a vacation—not so much as a single Saturday off.

She'd tried not to love Rafael. She'd tried. But somehow, he'd snuck past all her defenses….

Rafael's hand stroked her cheek. "You won't answer. You never answer," he said softly. "Someday you will." He looked down at her. "Someday, you will tell me everything."

But as he pulled her once more into his arms beneath the bright Greek sun, Louisa knew she would never tell him about the last man she'd fallen in love with. Her last boss. At least, she'd thought it was love at the time. She'd been so young then, so young and naive…

Thinking of the pain in her past, she looked at her future and was very, very afraid.

"Do you like this place?" he said softly, twisting a tendril of her hair around his finger.

She looked at him.

"So much that maybe I should get a job here," she said, only half-joking. "Does your friend who owns this island need a house-keeper? What is his name?"

Rafael glowered at her. Irritation emanated off him in waves.

"He is not a kind man. Especially where women are concerned."

She'd been trying to lighten the mood, but it seemed to have failed miserably. Why was he taking her comment so seriously? Lifting herself on one elbow, Louisa reached up to rub his shoulder. "The same could be said about you," she teased.

His jaw clenched. "Yes," he said shortly. "It could."

Was it possible he was jealous? No, surely not! "You know I'm not serious, Rafael!"

"I do not care for such jokes of you men-tioning other men," he said stiffly. "You belong to me."

She stopped rubbing his shoulder. She looked at him. "I belong to you?"

He shook his head. "You know what I meant. You are a valued member of my staff. You—"

"No," she interrupted. She pulled back her hand, sitting up. Suddenly she was so furious she couldn't think straight. "You had it right the first time. You think I *belong* to you. That you own me. That I'm your possession." So much for imagining herself to be his adored mistress! "You think I have no feelings." She slapped down on the nearby table. "Like this!"

"Do not be dramatic. I pay you well. There is no question of you being my possession. You stay in my employ because you appreciate your situation."

"And now?" She looked around them at the luxurious place that had suddenly lost its glamour. "Am I *working* for you now?"

He ground his teeth. "No. You know you are not!"

"Then who am I to you?"

"Here, you are my mistress. Beyond this island, you are the best servant on my staff. You oversee all of my homes, coordinating with the other housekeepers. I could not manage without you."

He might as well have slapped her across the face.

"Perhaps it really is time for me to move on," she said slowly, feeling numb. Why did she feel so betrayed, when she'd known all along how this would end?

"No," he said furiously. "You won't go work for him—or any other man. You belong to—*with*," he corrected himself as he caught her glare, "me."

His hands grasped her naked waist in the bright sunlight. She looked down into his gray eyes. His face was dark, almost savage. She could hear the hoarseness of his breath. Their eyes locked.

His fingers tightened on her almost painfully.

Then he reached up and kissed her.

His kiss was hard and deep, a plundering of her mouth, as if he'd held something back for far too long, as if the master had himself been enslaved by an unwilling passion he could no longer control. His kiss abruptly became more persuasive, wistful and sensual in a way she could not resist. She wrapped her arms around his neck as, with a low growl, he pulled her back against his naked body on the lounge chair. She could feel how he already wanted her again.

"You belong to me," he whispered. "Say it."

"Never," she said.

But her defiance only seemed to increase the force of his passion. He made love to her again beneath the hot Greek sun, hard and fast and with a brutality that matched her own passionate desire.

"You're the only woman I trust," he said in a low voice afterward, caressing her cheek as he looked down at her cradled in his arms. "The only woman I've trusted in a long, long time."

But as he held her and closed his eyes, dozing in the sun, tears streaked unheeded down Louisa's sunburned cheeks.

She was well and truly caught.

She had to face it. Though she knew it was nothing more than a fantasy, though she knew it was foolish, stupid and dangerous, she could no more stop loving him than stop breathing. No two-day idyll would cure her of loving Rafael.

She did belong to him. Completely.

CHAPTER FOUR

BACK in Istanbul the next afternoon, Louisa stumbled as she came out of the private hospital northeast of Taksim Square. Blindly she stepped into the street.

A loud honk made her fall back as she was nearly run over by a taxi driver who shouted at her in fluent, expressive Turkish. Gasping, almost crying, Louisa stood trembling on the sidewalk, shivering with shock.

Pregnant.

She was pregnant with Rafael's baby. Pregnant with the child she'd promised him she could never conceive!

Over the last week, she'd tried to mock her own fears, tried to convince herself she was being foolish to worry. But she hadn't been foolish at all. The doctor had just confirmed her worst fears had been right on target.

What would Rafael say when she told him?

She walked down the street, took deep breaths until she stopped trembling, then climbed back into the tiny car that was used by the staff. She drove north through the thick traffic to the outskirts of Beyoğlu.

They'd been back in Istanbul for only a few hours, but already everything had changed between them. Rafael had immediately gone to his home office and barked out orders to various assistants about the upcoming real estate deal he was hoping to have signed tonight. And all the house staff had rushed to her with their questions about the final preparations for the dinner party.

Louisa had become his employee again. Rafael had become her boss.

They'd left the lovers behind on the island. Left them behind forever.

Now, Louisa stared out at the busy traffic, colorful billboards and old buildings of the city through the grimy glass. The car needed to be washed, she thought dimly. She'd have to tell the chauffeur's assistant when she got back….

Should she even tell Rafael she was pregnant?

Her great-aunt's words came back to her. *Always be honest, child. Tell the truth, even if it hurts. Better to hurt now than twice as much later.*

But Louisa wasn't so sure. She'd saved five years of her salary in Europe, since she'd never taken time to travel or see the sights. She'd always told herself she mustn't be selfish—Mr. Cruz's needs must come first. She'd told herself she would see the sights of Europe later. Somehow, that time had never come.

And what did she have to show for it? She was just five years older. Pregnant. Alone!

The shaking vibration of the little car as she drove north on the old road was hypnotic.

Pregnant.

As she drove past the mansion's gate, she barely noticed the security guard's respectful greeting. She parked the car, informed the chauffeur's assistant that the car needed attention, then went into the house.

Everything looked beautiful for Rafael's birthday dinner tonight. Every room was filled with flowers, autumn roses from the garden supplemented with pepperberry stems and dark orange Asiatic lilies. As this was his first dinner party at his home in Istanbul, Louisa had planned it with care, choosing a menu rich with the exotic flavors of the city. Even now, the Turkish cook, who'd fortunately recovered from his earlier illness, was rushing around the kitchen and barking orders to his assistants to prepare the *midye dolmasi,* mussels stuffed with spiced rice, the sea bass stew, lamb kebabs and a variety of fruits and pastries for dessert.

She herself had made one of the desserts. It was not a traditional Turkish recipe, so it did not fit in with the menu, but she knew it was Rafael's favorite and so she'd made it that morning anyway. For his birthday. Because she loved him. It had taken her an hour, but she'd carefully prepared her specialty dessert, caramel macadamia brownies with white chocolate chips.

She'd wanted to make his first dinner here special. But since he intended to put the house on the market tomorrow, it would also be his last. Now, looking around her, she felt a lump in her throat.

She'd wanted everything to be perfect for

him. She'd made his home beautiful, made his life comfortable and full of ease. She'd sacrificed her every need for his. And now it was over. Now it was done. Once she told him she was pregnant, she would lose everything.

The job she loved. The man she loved.

Where would she go, without him to be both her albatross and her star? What would she do without him, all alone?

Slowly, heavily, she started to go up the stairs to her room. As she passed the study, she heard one of his assistants say, "Mademoiselle Lepetit is on the phone for you, sir."

Louisa froze on the stair.

Dominique Lepetit was a beautiful French starlet famous mostly for her time spent pouting while topless, posing for the paparazzi during the Cannes Film Festival. Blond, curvaceous and cruel—she was everything that most men seemed to want in a woman.

"Tell her I'm busy," came Rafael's curt reply, and Louisa exhaled. She hadn't realized until then how very much, in spite of everything, she wanted him to be faithful to her.

Rafael Cruz, faithful to any woman? She mocked herself as she climbed slowly up the stairs to her room. Had the pregnancy hormones kicked in already? She must really be out of her mind!

But he'd refused Dominique Lepetit's phone call. Could a man change?

Could he understand that sometimes fate changed people's lives in unexpected ways—for the better?

When she reached her room, she closed the door behind her, leaning against it for strength. She looked down in wonder, putting her hands on her belly as a new realization occurred to her.

Pregnant. A new life was growing inside her—Rafael's child. A smile lifted her lips. A *baby.* A sweet-smelling baby to cuddle in her arms, to love forever. Her parents had died long ago, and she'd been estranged from her younger sister for five years. But with this baby, she would finally have a family of her own. A reason to create a real home, after so many years alone.

Had Katie felt like this when she'd first found out she was pregnant?

Louisa pushed away the unbidden thought.

She didn't want to think about Katie. Didn't want to think about the niece or nephew she'd never met. The child must be almost five now, probably with brothers and sisters. And Matthias Spence as their father...

She'd tried not to think about Matthias for years. But to her surprise, the thought of him no longer hurt her the same way. Because she'd never really cared about him? She'd worked for him for only a few months before he'd proposed to her. She hadn't known him half so well as she knew Rafael.

Or perhaps it was because her relationship with Matthias seemed so laughably in the past, the crush of a schoolgirl long ago, compared to the enormity of being pregnant with Rafael's baby.

How could she tell Rafael the news?

Straightening her shoulders, Louisa went to her closet. She pushed through all the plain, serviceable clothes and pulled something out of the back, covered by plastic. Taking it out, she stared down at a sexy black bustier dress.

The last time she'd worn this, she'd been an engaged woman. Her sister had been visiting for a month from college, and had insisted they go shopping. "You're so lucky," Katie had said wistfully. "Going from a live-in housekeeper to a rich man's wife." "I love him," Louisa had replied, smiling. But she'd allowed Katie to talk her into spending an entire paycheck in one splurge on the dress for their engagement party. Louisa had hoped to look pretty for Matthias, and try her best to impress his friends. Then a few weeks later, an hour before their engagement party began, her nineteen-year-old sister had asked to speak to her privately.

"How could you?" Louisa had gasped a few moments later. "You're my sister. How could you do this to me?"

"I'm sorry!" Katie had cried. "I never meant to get pregnant. But I can't believe you even love him. If you did, you wouldn't have kept him at arm's length, refusing to sleep with him until you were married! Who does that anymore?"

"I do," Louisa had choked out, and grabbing her purse, she'd run from the house. She'd run as far away from Miami as she could, all the way to Paris.

She'd nearly thrown the dress in the trash five years ago. But instead, for some reason, she'd kept it. Now, the sexy black dress was the one item of clothing from her old life, before she'd been afraid of love, before she'd disappeared from the world to walk the earth like a ghost.

As she put on the dress, Louisa told herself she had no illusions that Rafael would love her; he would certainly never marry her. She only prayed he might love and accept their coming child. And that was the reason—the only reason!—that she put it on.

It was a little loose from her weight loss over the last few years, all the time she'd spent without time to exercise or sit down and eat meals or take care of herself properly. But when she added a belt, the dress still looked nice. She brushed her dark hair, leaving it tumbling and lustrous down her shoulders. She took off her black-rimmed plastic glasses and put in contact lenses. She was out of practice after wearing glasses for so long. She added some mascara to her lashes and some deep red lipstick on her mouth, then surveyed herself in the mirror for the effect.

After so many years, she almost didn't recognize herself.

She looked pretty.

Louisa prayed it would help. Because she was terrified.

As she went downstairs, she could hear the first guests starting to arrive outside. She saw Rafael at the base of the stairs and stopped, gripping the polished wood of the railing. She closed her eyes as she took a single calming breath, her hand on her belly. Could this night be anything like her deepest dreams?

"I'm pregnant, Rafael," she would say.

His gray eyes would widen. He'd gasp. Then he'd take her into his arms. "I am glad," he'd say fiercely. "Of course I want this baby. And I want you. You are the only woman for me, querida." *Looking down at her, he would lift her chin and whisper tenderly, "I love you, Louisa."*

"Louisa."

She opened her eyes to see Rafael looking up at her from the bottom of the stairs. He was frowning at her as if she'd dyed her hair purple and dressed like the Easter bunny.

"Why are you dressed like that?" he demanded, coldly surveying her from head to toe.

It wasn't quite the reaction she'd been

hoping for, but she tried to smile as she walked down the stairs—carefully, on her four-inch black patent high heels.

"For the party," she said. She stopped one step above him. He still wouldn't smile back at her. "For your birthday," she tried again.

Instead of looking pleased, Rafael scowled. "You are going to attract attention like that."

A servant should always be invisible. The rule had been drummed into her for ten months. After her parents had died, Louisa had given up her chance at a college scholarship to stay home and take care of her little sister and ailing great-aunt. But her aunt had left Louisa a small inheritance, which she'd used to attend butler school to become a certified household manager. *You are not a person to your employer. You are a tool in his service. Serve invisibly. Never invade your employer's privacy or force yourself upon his notice. To do so will cause embarrassment to you both.*

Now, Louisa stiffened. "You don't like my dress?"

He glared at her. "No."

It seemed almost impossible to believe just

that morning, she'd been in his arms. They'd been naked together in the amazing Greek mansion overlooking the Aegean. Now, when she needed his attention the most, he'd suddenly become distracted. Distant.

Was he already thinking about Dominique Lepetit, who was already on her way? Had he already forgotten Louisa completely?

"Go change," he said coldly. "The guests will arrive any moment."

He seemed completely disinterested in her. Just as he'd promised two days ago, their little affair had apparently cured his desire for her. He'd had his fill of her. He was done. He was ready to move on.

With a deep breath, she told herself it was irrelevant if he cared for her. She had to think about their unborn child. Rafael had to know she was pregnant. *For their baby's sake.*

As he turned to leave, she grabbed his wrist. It took every ounce of her courage. "I need to talk to you."

He stared at her hand on his wrist. She released him as if he'd burned her.

"I want you on the plane to Buenos Aires tomorrow," he replied icily.

"Buenos Aires?" she whispered, staggered. He no longer wanted her in Paris? "Why Buenos Aires?"

"You'll take over my house there." He gave a single dismissive nod, already turning away. "Now go change your dress."

Louisa felt a stab of pain.

He could not have said it more plainly. He no longer saw her as anything but a servant.

And the truth was that even in Greece, when she'd imagined herself his cosseted mistress, she'd still been his servant. Serving his needs in bed, rather than in the household. And now that he was done with her, he expected her to simply return to being invisible, to being the plain gray ghost that vanished into the hundred-year-old woodwork of the mansion.

So he cared nothing for her but as his invisible servant? She gritted her teeth.

So be it.

She had no intention of going to Buenos Aires. She wouldn't go meekly off to serve him forever in exile, while he enjoyed a succession of other women!

Having him love her—what a ridiculous fantasy that had been!

Her head pounded. She felt almost physically sick. But she pushed the pain aside. She would deal with that later. Tonight, she had a job to do.

She'd make his dinner party perfect. He would never have reason to complain she'd been anything less than an exemplary housekeeper.

Then, afterward, she would tell him she was accidentally pregnant. Not because she still hoped he might care. But because her baby deserved a father, and Rafael deserved the truth. He deserved that much, and no more.

The doorbell rang, and she lifted her chin.

"I'm sorry, your guests are already arriving," she said sweetly. "I have no time to change my clothes. Excuse me."

Pushing past him, she opened the door.

That night, as the guests arrived, Louisa personally stood near the door to take their coats. The house was all in readiness; she'd supervised everything. As she took each coat, she saw that each guest was more powerful, wealthy and beautiful than the last. She watched Rafael greet each of them, some with handshakes, some with slaps on the back.

But not the women—no. He greeted each of them with a kiss on both cheeks. The five women were all so beautiful, and every single one of them looked up at Rafael with longing. No wonder. Impeccably dressed in a tuxedo with a black tie, he was beyond handsome. He was the spectacular angel of his namesake.

He didn't look at Louisa. He seemed not to notice she was there, any more than he noticed the grandfather clock or the antique hat rack that she'd lovingly chosen for this mansion. All his possessions, *including her,* were to be used and then discarded at will when he no longer found them useful.

She clenched her hands, trying to ignore the pain.

"Dominique," he purred, pushing past Louisa to help the beautiful blond starlet remove her white fur coat. He pulled it off her shoulders himself, smiling down at her seductively. "I am glad to see you."

"Rafael." The infamous French beauty reminded Louisa of a pampered white Persian cat, with her tiny button nose, big blue eyes and fluffy bleached-blond hair. Her sparkly gold minidress barely covered her nipples on the top and upper thighs on the hemline. She smiled up at him with her curved red lips. "I wouldn't miss your birthday, *chéri.*"

Looking at them together, Louisa suddenly felt how plain she was, how tall and ungainly and skinny in her five-year-old black dress. A sharp pain rose in her throat. Twenty minutes earlier, she'd thought she looked rather pretty in the mirror but now she felt as drab as a sparrow. Why hadn't she just stayed in her gray smock and glasses? At least then no one would have snickered at the plain girl who was actually trying to look pretty, who was apparently under the delusion she could compete with someone like Dominique Lepetit!

Rafael and Dominique were suited for each other in every way, both physically and by reputation. The French starlet was as well-known for discarding love-tortured suitors as Rafael was known for crushing women's hearts. Louisa swallowed, looking down at the floor.

Suddenly a fur coat was thrust into her arms. She nearly coughed at the weight and

sensation of something so huge and fluffy—
like a dead animal beneath her nose.

"Take care of that, won't you?" Rafael
murmured to Louisa, not looking away from
Dominique.

"Of course, Mr. Cruz," she replied miserably.

The dinner party was sparkling. The company was served *mezes,* starters like stuffed
vine leaves and dip, cooked artichokes and
hummus with *pide* bread, along with cocktails and Argentinian wine. Louisa supervised the entire night, calming down the chef
who though recovered from his earlier illness,
seemed dangerously unhinged emotionally
as he rushed around the kitchen. Realizing
how many famous people were sitting in the
dining room for Rafael's birthday, the man
seemed to abruptly disintegrate under pres-
sure and, while shouting at one of his poor
assistants, he nearly cut the end of his thumb
off with a sharp knife.

She'd prepared for this. She'd gone to the
famous butler school in Miami when she'd
realized she had no skills except taking care
of people. And organizing homes. And, she
thought dully, falling in love with her boss.

Louisa managed the cook, calmed down the kitchen and then organized the waiters who brought out each course of the meal. Each time she went into the dining room she was involuntarily dazzled by the beautiful guests, by their sparkling conversations and witty repartee. She tried not to listen, but she could not help it. Just as she could not help noticing how Rafael looked into Dominique Lepetit's lovely, wicked eyes with such apparent fascination as they leaned their heads together and she whispered something in his ear.

She'd known Rafael would move on—but she'd never thought it would be at such lightning speed!

She swallowed, feeling increasingly hot as she returned to the kitchen. How could she tell him she was pregnant?

Should she even tell him?

What if he rejected their baby? What if he not only blamed Louisa for the pregnancy, but he was never able to love the child they'd created, the child he'd never wanted?

As the interminable dinner was finally drawing to an end, she went into the dining room and announced heavily that dessert and coffee would be awaiting them on the terrace. When one of the toothpick-skinny actresses asked her to list the desserts Louisa couldn't stop herself from looking at Rafael when she mentioned the caramel macadamia brownies. Across the room, from where he sat beside Dominique Lepetit, Rafael's slate-gray eyes suddenly locked with hers.

The pouting French beauty abruptly knocked over her wineglass. "Oh! *Mon dieu,* but how clumsy of me!"

With an intake of breath, Louisa hurried forward with a hand towel to clean up the mess. She saw Dominique's feline smile as the beautiful girl leaned forward on the table, blocking Rafael's gaze from her.

One of the other guests, a very handsome dark-eyed man sitting across the table, watched the scene with interest. As Louisa straightened from the table with hot, flushed cheeks and the wine-soaked towel, her eyes met the stranger's. His lips curved, as if he knew everything. Her cheeks, already red with humiliation, became hotter still.

"Novros," Rafael said, rising from the table

with sudden sharpness. "We have business to discuss. It is time."

"Yes," the other man said to him, his black eyes gleaming.

"Excuse us," Rafael said more smoothly to the other guests at the table, pausing for a particular smile at Dominique. "We will join you on the terrace in a moment. Miss Grey, will you show them the way, if you please?"

"Of course, sir," Louisa said over the lump in her throat.

Once outside in the moonlit night, upon the high stone terrace overlooking the garden and the sparkling Bosphorus below, the guests scattered in pairs into the shadows. Louisa directed several maids in setting up the pastries, including the *kadayif,* the shredded puff pastry filled with nuts and honey, along with strong Turkish coffee, brandy and other liqueurs, serving them on sterling silver trays filled with antique copper goblets.

As the maids bustled around her, Louisa paused in the moonlight. Blinking fast, she stared up into the inky-blackness of the sky twinkling with distant frozen stars.

Just yesterday, she'd been his mistress. Just

yesterday, she'd been free. Just yesterday, she'd had everything she'd ever wanted.

A lot could change in just one day.

By early autumn next year, she would be a mother. She would have a baby to love and care for.

But would her child have a father? Would Rafael have any love for their baby—or would he just resent and despise the innocent child for being forced upon him?

A shudder went through her body. She was afraid she already knew. He did not want a wife. Did not want a child. She had been a fool to ever dream otherwise. Louisa stared across the garden, yearning to run away and not even give Rafael the chance to despise and abandon them.

Why had she not kept to her original plan and waited to become a wife, before she'd ever risked becoming a mother?

Because she'd been in love with Rafael for years. And at twenty-eight years old, she hadn't felt principled and idealistic. Her virginity had started to feel like a burden. She'd started to feel like she would never be wanted—never be loved.

She took a deep breath when she heard

the guests flirting and laughing among each
other out in the shadows of the garden. As
soon as she could get Rafael alone, she would
be the idealistic, principled girl that she'd
been raised to be. She would be strong. She
would force herself to tell him the truth, even
if it did nothing but hurt her.

Wouldn't she?

Rafael was in hell.

He'd been distracted all night. By returning
to Istanbul. By his guests. By his birthday.
By the business deal he was about to make.

Most of all, by Louisa.

He was trying his damnedest to push her
away. To keep her at a distance. He was desperate to return to simply being boss and
employee. He'd promised her it would be
easy, hadn't he? He'd promised her when
they returned to Istanbul, everything would
fall back into place. But his plan that never
before failed—had failed.

Somehow, after two days of making love
to her, he still wanted her more than ever.

And if that weren't bad enough, Louisa
had come down the stairs looking like some
kind of damned sex symbol in a tight black

dress. Was she trying to torture him? Or was it possible…she already knew his plan had failed, and so she was looking for a new employer?

His hands tightened. From the moment he'd seen her in that dress, he'd hated the thought of any other man looking at her. One man above all—his business rival, Xerxes Novros. He'd invited his Greek rival to the party in his determination to finally close the real estate deal in Paris; but the two men were far from friends. Novros was such a callous womanizer, he made Rafael look like a damned saint. That was why Rafael had ordered Louisa to change clothes before the party. When she'd come down the stairs, looking so shockingly, glamorously beautiful in a way he'd never seen her before, he knew at once that she would attract the wrong attention.

"By the way," the Greek said coolly as they walked down the hall, "I never wished you a happy birthday."

"Thanks." At thirty-seven, Rafael no longer felt young and invincible. His soul was starting to feel brittle around the edges. He was ready to leave this city, with his failure and the memory of his father's funeral, far behind him.

Rafael had hundreds, perhaps thousands, of friends around the world. They were amusing. They were witty. The women were beautiful and eagerly gave themselves to his bed. The men were all business rivals who placed bets and smiled through their teeth like wolves. He didn't really give a damn about any of them, including the guests who were here tonight. He craved distraction.

He craved...*her.*

"You have a beautiful house," Xerxes Novros said as he followed Rafael down the hall to his private study. "You said your housekeeper supervised the refurbishment? That lovely creature in the sexy black dress?"

"Yes," Rafael growled as he snapped on the light. He closed the door behind them then picked up papers from his desk. "Your lawyers sent their corrections this morning. Sign these and we'll be done."

"Does she have a lover?"

"Who?"

"Your housekeeper."

"None of your damned business."

Flashing him a smile, Novros flung himself down in a high-backed chair and looked idly through the contract.

Rafael sat down at his desk, watching him. He never should have borrowed the man's private Greek island the last two days, he thought grimly. It gave him the vague sense of being in the man's debt. A dangerous feeling as he finished the negotiations of purchasing the real estate in Paris, a prestige property in the business district of La Défense. A dangerous feeling, as it brought Louisa to the other man's notice.

"It all appears to be in order." Novros looked up with a lazy smile. "Throw in your housekeeper to seal the bargain, and we have a deal."

Rafael's hand tightened on his pen.

"Careful," he growled through his teeth. He lifted his head, and his eyes glittered dangerously at his rival. "Don't talk about her. Don't even look at her."

Novros lifted a dark eyebrow. "I see," he said mildly, and looked back at the papers. He shook his head and threw them back on his desk. "Sorry. I'm going to need more time to think about it."

Rafael clenched his jaw. He needed to break ground on the hugely expensive property at once in order to meet his schedule, and they both knew it. He wished to build a new headquarters for his international conglomerate in Paris. They'd already agreed on a price. He was tempted to smash the man's face in.

Instead he smiled.

"Shall we throw in a sweetener?" Rafael suggested. "Sign it. Finish the deal. And this house—" he indicated the study with a generous sweep of his hand "—will be thrown into the bargain."

Xerxes Novros stared at him for a moment.

Then with a nod, he signed the papers with a flourish.

"You gave in too easily," the man said, handing the contract back to Rafael with an insolent grin. "I would have accepted less money for the property in Paris."

Rafael took the signed contract and put it in his safe. "And I would have sold this house for a single euro."

The other man stared at him, then snorted. "So we've both done well, then." He lifted his chin, looking around the study. "How long will it take your people to get your possessions out of my house?"

"A week."

"Fine." Novros rose to his feet, then stopped at the door. "I suppose your little housekeeper is the mistress you took to my island?"

Rafael tensed. It irritated him that the man guessed that—and that he'd even noticed Louisa! "You find that so hard to believe?"

"Not now that I've seen her." Novros paused, then said evenly, "Just be careful."

"What?"

"With her history."

Rafael stared at him. Novros knew something about Louisa that he, Rafael, did not? "What about it?" he bit out.

"Do you not know? Your Miss Grey used to work for a friend of mine in Miami. She lured him on, got an engagement ring out of him by keeping him out of her bed. Then when he started to lose interest, she invited her younger sister to come stay with them. The sister immediately seduced him into her bed. He was so sex-starved, he didn't even think to use a condom. She got pregnant, as they'd planned, and the man felt he was honor-bound to marry her." An admiring grin spread across his lips. "It was quite a clever plan, really."

A cold chill went down Rafael's spine.

"I'm just telling you this," Novros said casually, "from one free bachelor to another. Be careful."

Rafael felt cold. Then hot.

This was Louisa's secret? This was the big mystery of her past? Something so sordid— and clichéd—as gold diggers getting their hands into wealthy men by deliberately trapping them with a pregnancy?

He sucked in his breath as he remembered calling to check Louisa's references. Of course her employer's wife had given Louisa an excellent reference. The woman he'd spoken with was her *sister!*

"Get her pregnant, and she'll play you for a fool," Novros said lazily. He stroked the polished wood of the door frame thoughtfully. "She did do excellent work overseeing this house. A very clever girl—and beautiful to boot. Send her to me, won't you, when you're tired of her?"

After the man left, Rafael sat still at his

desk, staring blankly at the wallpaper across the study.

Louisa had said she was on the Pill. He'd blindly believed her. He'd told himself Louisa Grey would never tell a lie. He, who trusted no woman, had trusted her!

Cold rage slowly built up inside him. Was everything Novros had said true? Had Louisa been *trying* to become pregnant?

She'd had ample opportunity. He hadn't used a condom in Greece, either. In fact, she could already be pregnant now.

Placing his hands on his desk, he pushed himself to his feet. He took a deep breath, briefly closing his eyes as he clenched his fists. Then he went out into the garden.

He found Dominique waiting for him in the moonlight, pouting and smiling.

"Darling, I've been waiting for you for so long," she purred. She shimmied toward him in her tiny gold dress. She reached up her arms, barely able to reach his shoulders as she gave a seductive laugh. "It took you so long."

Coldly he pushed her away.

"Go home, Dominique," he said. "The party is over."

And leaving the pampered French starlet gaping behind him, he strode toward the terrace, where he saw the source of his desire, his suffering and his fury. *Louisa.*

CHAPTER FIVE

COLORFUL paper lanterns swung across the trees in the breeze, illuminating the dark garden above the black shimmer of the Bosphorus far below as Louisa cleaned the dishes from the terrace.

Dessert was over. Most of the guests had swiftly disappeared, returning to their rented villas or to nearby hotels, gorgeous women and wealthy men pairing off, seduced by each other and the exotic sensuality of Istanbul.

Louisa looked up when she heard a trill of low, feminine laughter. Dominique Lepetit's laughter. She heard the murmur of Rafael's low voice in answer.

For a moment, Louisa stared out blindly into the night. She blinked back cold tears beneath the cool breeze of wind coming off the water.

Then with a deep breath, she bent over to continue scrubbing the stone table. She gathered the silver coffeepot and dirty dishes back onto a tray. Some of the puff pastries remained, but all of her specialty caramel-macadamia brownies had been devoured down to the last crumbs. Rafael had never gotten his birthday brownie after all….

Louisa heard footsteps on the terrace and looked up.

A tall, dark-haired man stood alone on the other side of the terrace. He looked her over with an appreciative glance.

"You are Miss Grey?"

"Yes."

"I enjoyed those bars you made. What were they?"

She swallowed. "My secret recipe."

"A secret. How delightful." He wasn't entirely handsome; he had a slightly crooked nose, and a cruel twist to his lips as he said carelessly, "And if I offered to pay you a million dollars?"

She lifted her chin. "I still wouldn't give it to you. It's mine."

For a moment, he stared at her. Then he smiled. "Good for you."

And with those incomprehensible words, the man left her. She stared after him for a moment, frowning as she lifted the tray full of all the dirty dishes, whiskey and brandy bottles and small plates of half-eaten desserts.

"What did he say to you?"

Rafael's voice was harsh behind her.

Louisa almost dropped the tray as she whirled around. He took the tray from her grasp and set it back down on the stone table. His gray eyes flashed.

"What did Novros say?" Rafael demanded in a low, dangerous voice.

She shook her head, frowning in confusion. "Nothing."

"You're lying. I heard him speak to you. Did he offer you a job?" He grabbed her wrists and suddenly the expression on his handsome face was so hard and full of repressed fury, she felt afraid. "Did he offer you something more?"

Bewildered at his strange reaction, she shook her head. "No."

"Then what?" he demanded.

She swallowed. "He didn't make sense."

His grip tightened on her. "Tell me," he ordered.

She whispered, "He offered me a million dollars for my brownie recipe, then when I wouldn't, he just said… 'Good for you.'"

Rafael's jaw clenched. His impossibly handsome face looked like stone in the moonlight.

"Do you know what he meant?" she asked.

With a coldly furious expression, he shook his head.

She licked her lips nervously. Why was Rafael acting so angry? She felt a lump in her throat, a nausea right beneath her ribs.

He wouldn't release her wrist, and a hard knot of anger grew in her own throat. She thought she'd known him—known all his faults. But she'd never seen Rafael so dark, so altogether brutal.

Ripping her hand away, she demanded, "Why are you acting like this?"

"You know why," he growled.

Grasping at straws, she asked, "Did something happen to your business deal, Mr. Cruz?"

His lips twisted into a harsh, ironic smile

at the *Mr. Cruz.* "An interesting suggestion. It's always about money to you, isn't it?"

He wasn't making any sense—any more than that Greek man had! Louisa's hand tightened into a fist as she picked up the wet, dirty towel she'd been using to scrub the stone table. She took a deep breath. "Miss Lepetit is no doubt looking for you."

"Miss Lepetit," he ground through his teeth, "is gone. All the other guests have gone. We are—" his lips curved "—alone."

"Oh," she whispered, licking her suddenly dry lips. So this was her chance, then. Possibly her only chance to tell him she was pregnant…

But how could she tell him now, when he was acting so dark and strange?

She twisted the wet towel in her hands as she looked up at him nervously. "There's something I need to tell you, Rafael," she whispered. "It's important."

He grabbed her shoulders. Startled, she dropped the towel heavily against the stone terrace floor.

"What is it?" he demanded in a low voice.

She sucked in her breath, searching his

gaze. Did he already know she was pregnant? Had he somehow guessed?

She licked her lips. "It's not something I thought could happen. I denied it, even to myself…"

"Let me guess," he said sardonically. "You're desperately in love with me."

She nearly gasped. Then, looking up into his face, she told him the truth.

"Yes," she whispered.

His face hardened. "For so long, you've been such a mystery. An intriguing problem to solve." He brushed back tendrils of her dark hair the wind had blown across her face. "But now I understand you. At last."

She shivered beneath his touch, closing her eyes.

Was it possible that everything she'd dreamed of for so long was about to happen? Was it possible he was about to tell her he loved her as well, and in a moment, when she told him shyly about their coming baby, he would take her into his arms and kiss her?

She could barely breathe….

"You've been setting me up," he said harshly. "Just like you and your sister did with your last employer."

Her eyes flew open.

"My...my sister?"

She felt Rafael's fingers clench into her shoulders, and she gasped. He looked down at her with something close to hatred in his eyes.

"I thought I could trust you," he said in a low voice. "But it was all just a trick, wasn't it?"

"No," she whispered. She shook her head. "You're wrong."

He gave a harsh, cruel laugh.

"I trusted you. Trusted you as I trusted no other woman alive. But have you spent the last five years of your life setting me up for a con?"

"What?" she gasped. Unshed tears stung her eyes as she shook her head fiercely. "I don't—"

"Tell me the truth!" he said coldly. "Was I a fool to trust you? *Did you lie when you said you were on the Pill?*"

Horrified, Louisa sucked in her breath.

For a moment, silence fell. The cool breezes from the sea caused the colorful paper lanterns to sway amid the darkness of the garden.

Rafael's jaw was set in a grim line as his hands tightened on her.

"I thought I'd done due diligence by calling your last employer personally. I spoke to his wife, not realizing she was your *sister*. Of course she gave you a glowing recommendation—she wanted to help you get your wealthy man, as you helped her!"

Louisa drew back, tears suddenly in her eyes as she thought of all the pain. "That's not how it was!"

"No?" His lip curled. "Then how was it?"

Louisa took a deep breath. She didn't want to speak of the past, but she had no choice. For their child's sake, she had to make him understand that her pregnancy was an accident—not a trap!

"Five years ago, I fell in love with my boss," she whispered, then stopped.

Rafael gripped her shoulders. "Go on."

"I'd only been working as his housekeeper for a few months when Matthias asked me to marry him." Every low, hoarse word felt painfully ripped from her. "But I wouldn't go to bed with him. I told him I wanted to wait for our wedding night. I was so young, so young and idealistic. Then my little sister came to visit from college." She looked up at him, blinking back tears. "The night of our engagement party, Katie told me Matthias was going to marry her instead. Because... she was pregnant with his baby."

Staring down at her, he took a deep, shuddering breath. For a moment, she thought he meant to comfort her. Then his dark eyes looked at her with the fire of betrayal.

"Just as the two of you planned all along. You left him sex-starved, your sister lured him into her bed and he fell into her trap. Just as I fell into yours," he said in a low, cold voice. "I trusted you, Louisa. Although I should have suspected something when I first took you to bed. There would be no reason for a virgin with no boyfriend to be on the Pill—"

"I told you, it was for cramps, to regulate my cycle—"

"I thought it was just an unfortunate coincidence," he spoke over her ruthlessly, "that when I came home that night and found you crying in Paris, the apartment was out of condoms. You set me up so methodically, and I wanted you so badly, I was blind."

Louisa stared at him in shock and grief.

She'd shared something of her past she'd never spoken about with anyone—but he didn't give a damn. He was just determined to use her own words against her!

A slow burn of anger built inside her.

"I forgot to restock the condoms, but that wasn't on purpose! Perhaps I had trouble—" she lifted her chin defiantly "—because you were going through boxes so rapidly."

His jaw twitched. Abruptly releasing her, he folded his arms. "You lured me by acting distant, knowing that would intrigue me. Then you made sure I found you weeping, needing comfort, knowing there was only one kind of comfort I would offer."

"I never thought you would come home early from your date and seduce me!"

"So you're not pregnant?"

She sucked in her breath.

This was worse, so much worse than she'd thought. Why hadn't she realized that her two-day stomach flu had totally ruined the effectiveness of the birth control? She'd never thought he might look at her past and imagine that she could be so devilishly clever.

If she were, she thought bitterly, she

wouldn't have slept with a heartless, suspicious playboy like Rafael Cruz!

Dark shadows and swinging red lights moved over his hard expression, making him look devilish. She sucked in her breath, trembling at the dark promise she saw in his eyes. It made her take an involuntary step backward.

She had to lie. There was no way she could tell him the truth now.

But the thought of denying the existence of her unborn child, the weight of telling such an awful lie, beat down upon her like golf-ball-size chunks of ice.

She felt incredibly hormonal and exhausted from being pregnant and traveling back from Greece. She felt tearful and emotionally drained from the roller-coaster ride of the last few days. Just yesterday, she'd been his adored mistress; today, she'd been ripped apart by the discovery of her pregnancy, and yet she'd been forced to hide her emotion, to serve him and his fancy guests while watching him flirt with another woman.

And suddenly, she'd *had it*.

Louisa took a deep breath. Slowly she looked up at him. She could live without his love. She could ball up her heart into a block of ice. She could ignore her feelings. She'd done it before.

But he had to love their baby.

If Rafael was cold to their innocent child and treated him badly through his whole life, letting their son or daughter know they were never wanted… No, she couldn't let that happen. She would deny their child's existence before she would risk causing her baby such endless grief!

He gently stroked her cheek. But his gaze was anything but gentle as he raked her soul with his fury and rage. She had the sudden feeling of being trapped. His body, his darkness, towered over her.

The heat between them felt like a cold burn. Like ice. *Like a threat.*

"There's only one thing I need to know," Rafael said in a low voice. "One thing that will determine if I was a fool to believe you were the last honest woman on earth. So tell me." His dark eyes glittered in the swaying light of the red paper lanterns. "Are you pregnant, Louisa?"

* * *

Rafael's muscles were painfully tense as he waited for her answer.

She wouldn't meet his eyes.

"Could you love a baby?" she whispered.

He nearly growled at her. "Don't change the subject. Answer my question."

"If I accidentally got pregnant," she faltered, "don't you think it's possible it could have nothing to do with money, and everything to do with…with…"

"Love?" He sneered.

Wordlessly she nodded. Her eyes were wide, limpid pools in the night. Wild. Desperate.

For a moment, his body instinctively wished to comfort her. It was the same way he'd felt when she'd revealed how she'd loved her last boss then lost him—to her sister. He'd almost pulled her into his arms, until he'd reminded himself that this might be part of her con. Her innocence, her pain, her supposed *love*—was it all an act to get him to marry her?

His stomach clenched. "A mere housekeeper does not go to all the trouble of getting pregnant by a wealthy man without expecting a payout."

Turning pale, she gasped.

Then her lovely face hardened, in that aloof, cold expression he knew so well.

"So I'm a *mere housekeeper* now, am I?" she said in a low voice. Her dark eyes glittered. "Just what sort of payout do you think I want?"

He set his jaw. "Marriage."

She sucked in her breath. *"Marriage?"*

"You know very well," he said grimly, "if you were pregnant, I would have no other choice."

They stared at each other in the shadows of the garden.

Looking down at her beautiful face, Rafael's body hurt with tension and fury.

He'd always vowed he would never get trapped by any woman. It had happened to him once, and that was enough. At seventeen, he'd fallen for an older woman who'd callously dropped him to marry a wealthy man. When Rafael had pleaded with her to marry him instead, she'd laughed at his tiny diamond ring. The faded Cruz fortune wasn't nearly enough to tempt her, she'd said. She liked his body well enough, but money was what mattered most to her.

At eighteen, he'd made it his mission in life to get rich. Ten years later, he'd ruined the woman—and her husband—in payback.

Rafael would never feel desperate over a woman again. It was why he could never have children. He would never give a woman that kind of power over him. Never feel vulnerable again. *Never.*

He looked at Louisa. *Especially* her. She had too much power over him already.

Against his will, Rafael's gaze dropped to her lush mouth. Even now, wondering if she'd tricked him, wondering if she were the most accomplished liar he'd ever met, Rafael couldn't stop wanting to kiss her. His body ached for her.

"So if I were pregnant, you would really wish to marry me?" she whispered.

In spite of all her defiance, he saw that she wished to marry him. She wanted to pin him down. *She was no different from all the rest.*

He said evenly, "There's no way I would allow my child to be raised by some other man. So I would make you my wife. Is that what you want, Louisa?" he said dangerously. "Is that what you've wanted all along?"

With a deep intake of breath, she looked away from him, staring out at the view of Istanbul across the Bosphorus. So close across the water, but it was another continent entirely—Asia.

Clenching his hands into fists, he stared at her. Louisa was like that. So close, and yet so far. She was standing beside him. He could feel the warmth of her skin. And yet she was so far away. He realized he'd never really known her at all.

"Would you be a good father?" she whispered into the night, still not looking at him. "Would you love our child?"

His eyes narrowed as he looked at her lovely face, so different without glasses. Her eyes were wide and deep as the night. Her long dark hair brushed against her creamy shoulders in the soft breeze. She was the most beautiful, elusive woman he'd ever known. *And he hated her for her beauty.*

When he spoke, his voice was low and even.

"I would marry you for the baby's sake. But I would make you pay for trapping me into marriage," he continued in a low voice. He reached out and brushed a tendril of hair off her cheek with his fingertips. He felt her shiver beneath his touch as he leaned forward to whisper in her ear, "I would make you pay…and pay…and pay."

"What do you mean?" she gasped, shuddering.

He gave a cold, cruel smile as he straightened. "I would take pleasure of you in my bed until I had my fill." He stared down at her. "I would own you, as you would never own me."

She sucked in her breath.

She looked up at him, her eyes troubled in shadow. "But would you love our baby?"

Suddenly he was done with her endless evasions. Setting his jaw, he reached into his pocket for a cell phone. He dialed a number and spoke into the phone. "Dr. Vincent, please."

"What are you doing?"

He looked at her coldly. "Since you refuse to tell me if you're pregnant, I will have you examined by my doctor in Paris."

Louisa ripped the phone from his hands and ended the call. She took a deep breath.

"Well?" he said coolly.

"I'm…" She licked her lips.

He stared at her, his heart full of darkness and fury.

"I'm…" she said in a low voice. She took a deep breath, briefly closing her eyes as she said, "I'm not pregnant."

He exhaled in a rush. "You're not?"

She stared at him. Her eyes were pools of darkness.

Relief coursed through him, almost making him stagger.

He hadn't been wrong about her! She could be trusted! He hadn't been such a fool as he'd feared!

Then, staring at Louisa's tight shoulders and barely concealed fury, he reconsidered that statement. If she was innocent, he'd just treated her very badly indeed.

Looking at her with sudden regret, he rubbed the back of his head wryly. He'd let Novros's suspicions get to him. The Greek bastard had probably made it all up, he thought in irritation, spinning the facts for his own reasons, hoping to cause friction between Rafael and his housekeeper. Hoping he could get Louisa for himself!

He sighed. So who was a stupid fool after all…?

"Sorry," he said, spreading his hands wide and giving her his best smile. "Forgive me. I let my suspicions get the best of me. I should have known I could trust you, Louisa…"

But as he reached out for her shoulder, she backed away before he could touch her.

Rafael ground his teeth, silently cursing both his own untrusting nature and the Greek business rival who'd so easily managed to cause such trouble in his household.

"So, Miss Grey," he said in a determinedly jocular voice, "your housekeeping skills are desperately needed at my apartment in Buenos Aires. Please go fix it up, just as you've done here. There's no reason to stay in Istanbul any longer, as I just gave this house away in a business deal—"

"You did what?"

"You'll fly to Argentina in the morning. I will follow in a week or two, after I've completed the Paris deal."

For a moment, she was silent. Then she said a single cold word.

"No."

He tried again. "You will, of course, receive a much-deserved raise. I intend to double your salary."

"No," she bit out. She lifted her chin, and her eyes glittered. "I've done nothing, nothing to deserve the humiliating treatment you've given me. My only mistake was sleeping with a heartless playboy, knowing what kind of man you were!"

He set his jaw. "Louisa, you must believe I never meant—"

"I'm not finished!" she nearly shrieked. "For the last month, I've asked myself again and again how I could have slept with you in Paris. Then I did it again, letting you convince me to be your mistress on that Greek island. I wanted you so desperately. For years, I've made excuses for your bad behavior. I told myself you had some goodness deep inside you. I've devoted every moment of the last five years to making your life comfortable. But now, I see you how you really are. How could I have ever let myself love you? A cold-hearted, selfish bastard like you?"

"I never asked you to love me." He gritted his teeth. "And I paid you well—"

"You'll never pay me another penny," she interrupted in a low, cold fury. "I won't take one more dime from you. Ever."

He took a deep breath. "Louisa, you're just

upset," he said in a reasonable voice. "I admit I was rude to jump to conclusions, but surely you can see how your past looked to me? I am sorry I accused you of trying to trap me. I should have known you would never try to purposefully get pregnant with a child neither of us want. Forgive my stupidity," he said humbly. "Let's forget all this unpleasantness. Leave it behind and return to how we were. Boss. Valued employee."

She shook her head, her face a mask of repressed fury and some other emotion he could not read. Disgust? Grief?

"I will never work for you again," she whispered. "God help any woman stupid enough to be completely under your control. I'm done with you, Rafael. I never want to see you again." She lifted her chin, and her eyes glittered. *I quit.*

CHAPTER SIX

Sixteen months later

THE bakery had been busy all day amid the hubbub of the early spring season in Key West. Outside, the sun was warm, glimmering off the turquoise sea and a cruise ship docked nearby. It was only early afternoon, but Louisa guessed that she'd already served nearly every tourist on that ship. As she worked the counter, she glanced at the ship briefly through the storefront window that proclaimed Grey's Bakery.

Then, as the family of six left with their arms full of doughnuts and cookies, Louisa turned with an apologetic smile to the last customer. "Good afternoon. I'm so sorry for the wait—"

Then she finally got a good look at the man

who'd been behind the throng of tourists. She sucked in her breath. The tongs she'd been holding dropped to the floor with a clang.

Rafael looked down at her, smiling with his dark eyes.

"Hello, Louisa," he said. "How are you?"

She stared at him in shock, unable to speak.

It had been almost a year and a half since she'd left him in Istanbul, this selfish, cold-hearted man who hadn't wanted either a wife or a child. He looked at her now with the exact same gray shade of eyes as her baby son, who was now almost eight months old. The baby who was right now sleeping in the tiny office behind the counter. *The baby he didn't know about.*

Involuntarily she moved a little to the right, blocking his view of the office door. What was Rafael doing in Florida? Had he somehow found out about Noah?

"What are you doing here?" she choked out.

"You don't look pleased to see me." He rubbed the back of his dark hair and glanced up at her with a sheepish half smile. "I guess you're not the one who sent the letter. I hoped you were."

"Letter?" She hid her shock by leaning down behind the counter to pick up the tongs from the tile floor. She turned and dropped them into a sinkful of soapy water. Bracing her hands against the sink, she closed her eyes and took a deep breath.

"Not exactly a letter," he clarified. "It was a flyer advertising your bakery. Someone sent it to my office in Paris."

A chill went through her. She knew just who'd sent it. *Damn Katie!*

Fear pierced her heart.

Don't be afraid, she told herself desperately. Why should Rafael Cruz frighten her? She was no longer his employee. No longer his lover. This was her bakery, hers and her sister's, and if Louisa chose, she would throw him out onto the street!

He had no power over her, she told herself. None whatsoever.

But she knew that was a lie. She thought of her baby in the darkened room behind her. If he knew about Noah…

Could he possibly know?

Sucking in her breath, she turned to face him. Her eyes searched his face.

Then she exhaled. He didn't know. He couldn't. If he'd known, he wouldn't be looking at her with an expression that was so open and friendly and warm. He would have come in here with all guns blazing.

"What do you want, Rafael?" she bit out. She would never call him Mr. Cruz, ever again.

"I've missed those caramel brownies of yours," he said. "I'll pay for them, of course."

She heard the echo of his long-ago words. *I would make you pay…and pay…and pay.* She lifted her chin. "I thought I made it clear that I never wished to see you again."

"You did," he admitted. "But when I got that letter, I realized that I wanted to see you." He smiled at her. "Can we go somewhere to talk?"

The smile he gave her would have melted the heart of any woman.

But not hers. Never again. She glared at him, then turned with an elaborate smile to help a new customer who'd just come in her store. He waited with unusual patience as she served the other customer. After the tinkle of the bell as the customer went back onto the boardwalk with a bagful of doughnuts, Louisa finally turned to him coldly.

"I have nothing to say to you. Please leave."

"I had to find you, Louisa. To tell you," he said, "to tell you I'm…sorry."

She stared at him.

He was sorry.

"You have nothing to be sorry about," she said coldly. "I'm glad you forced me to quit. My life now is exactly what it should be." After she'd fled Istanbul, she'd returned to Miami, where she'd been stunned to discover Katie was a widow, living in a mobile home and barely able to support her five-year-old daughter. They'd hugged and cried in each others' arms. Now, they were sisters again. *They were a family.* Louisa lifted her chin. "You did me a favor."

He looked at her ruefully. "I did?"

Louisa nodded coldly. She'd used her savings to start this bakery on Key West, a place she'd visited long ago. This bakery wasn't just a family business, it was a labor of love. Even her little niece, who was now in first grade, helped out. The two sisters worked here during the day, and lived upstairs with their children in a small apartment above the bakery.

She had the perfect life now. She had her family, a successful business she loved and friends on this island. And if she still sometimes dreamed of Rafael, hot dreams of longing in the night—well, what of that? She didn't want him. She was better off without him!

Rafael looked at her. His eyes were as deep and dark as the Caribbean at midnight. He shook his head. "Ever since you left Istanbul, I've regretted my behavior that day. I never should have let my suspicions get the better of me."

"Forget it," she said shortly.

"I cannot." He looked at her regretfully, then with a sigh, he clawed back his dark hair. "I accused you of trying to get pregnant with my child. You! Of all women on earth, I should have known you would not do such a thing!"

She surreptitiously glanced back at the room where their baby was sleeping. She heard the soft snuffle of Noah's heavy breath.

He would be hungry and waking soon. Katie had gone to pick up her daughter from school, but any moment now she'd be back to take her turn working the counter.

Her interfering, well-meaning sister would no doubt be thrilled to see Rafael. *Curse her.*

"Forgive me," Rafael said humbly, bowing his head. "I am sorry for how badly I treated you."

She heard her baby shift in his playpen, heard his snuffle as he started to wake up.

"I forgive you," she said abruptly.

"Just like that?"

"Just like that." She had to get Rafael out of her bakery—fast. She moved behind the counter, using fresh tongs to pick up some of her caramel brownies, the most popular item at the bakery, and put them in a white bag. "Here," she said. "Take these as a peace offering. On the house."

"Thank you." He took the bag, but he did not leave as she'd hoped. Instead he hesitated, propping the bag on the side counter as he slowly looked around the shop. "It's a beautiful store."

"Thanks," she said unwillingly.

"How did you end up here? At this remote island?"

Not remote enough, she thought, looking at him. "My sister was still living in Miami with her daughter. Her husband had died the year before."

"Yes," he said quietly. "I just heard about that."

"Right." Matthias Spence, the handsome, wealthy older man the Grey sisters had once fought over, had died of a heart attack shortly after the government had seized his remaining fortune for milking his investors in a money-making scheme. "But we're all doing fine now."

"Really?" he said softly.

"Yes," she ground out. Except she was going to kill Katie for sending Rafael the flyer. Her sister had been pestering her for the last year to tell Rafael about Noah. Louisa folded her arms. How could Katie have gone behind her back like this?

"I'm glad you're doing well," Rafael said in a low voice. "You deserve to be happy."

"Yes." But her success came at a price. Between caring for the baby and the bakery, Louisa only slept six hours a night at most.

She was so tired. So, so tired. And Rafael looked more devilishly handsome than ever, well-rested and well-groomed in his black button-down shirt and slim-fitting jeans. "We work hard," she said. "Matthias left nothing to my sister. The bakery needs constant attention, as do the children."

"Children?" he asked.

Louisa bit her tongue, furious at her mistake. But before she could come up with an explanation, the bell chimed at the door.

"Sorry I'm late." Her sister came in with her niece, who was carrying a backpack and several large sheets of artwork. "The line at the school was so long. It seems all the parents wanted to pick up their kids today.... Oh." She stopped, staring at Rafael. "Hello."

Louisa glared at her. "Look who dropped by for a visit. My old boss."

Katie had the audacity to smile and hold out her hand. "Nice to meet you, Mr. Cruz."

"Call me Rafael."

"Rafael."

Behind them, Louisa simmered with fury. Then she jumped when she heard her baby give a soft mewling whimper from behind the office door. She glanced at Rafael, but by some miracle, he hadn't heard it. *Yet.*

"I think I'll give him a quick tour around the island," Louisa interrupted abruptly. She looked at Rafael. "Would you like that?"

He looked startled, but instantly said, "Yes."

Louisa untied her apron. "Take over the counter for me, Katie. Feed the little one with what I left in the fridge." She gave her sister a hard look. "I'll talk to you later."

Looking abashed, her sister nodded. Katie would make sure to feed Noah some of the milk she'd left in the fridge.

Hanging her apron up on a hook, Louisa came around the counter. Kicking off her sturdy shoes and shoving her feet into flip-flops, she pulled out her bun and shook out her hair, letting it tumble down her bare shoulders over her tank top. "Have you seen Key West?"

"No," he said, looking at her shoulders and hair. His gaze lifted slowly from her chest to her neck to her lips to her eyes. "When my plane landed, I came straight here."

"You're in for a treat," she said grimly. "Come with me."

Rafael couldn't stop looking at her.

Louisa had changed so much in sixteen months, he thought. How much had changed? Her hair? Her face? Her clothes? Yes, but it was more than that.

For the last year and a half, when he'd dreamed of Louisa, he'd pictured her either naked or in a gray shapeless skirt suit, wearing black glasses over her pale skin with her brown hair pulled back into a tight bun.

This new Louisa looked nothing like the tight, prim, aloof housekeeper he remembered.

Now, her face was tanned, bringing out the natural beauty of her bare face. He could see the intense color of her eyes in the sun. Her lips were deep pink. Her hair no longer was pulled back into the tight bun, but now fell down her shoulders, highlighted by the sun into the color of dark honey. She'd put on a few pounds in all the right places. His eyes traced the shape of her body beneath the aqua-colored tank top and madras shorts. What was different?

Color, he realized. She was in color.

She'd been beautiful as his employee, but had always been in the background, almost invisible, the capable Miss Grey in her black-framed glasses, sensible shoes and gray suit.

Here in this little town, on the edge of the turquoise Caribbean Sea, Louisa was vibrant with her youth and energy. She shone with color and life.

As they walked toward the beach, he couldn't take his eyes off her. He hadn't come just to ask for forgiveness. He'd come to offer Louisa her old job back. He'd missed her. His houses were all disorganized, half in shambles since she'd left. He'd intended to quadruple her salary, to give her two months of vacation a year, to invite her family to come along—whatever it took to lure her. He needed her. Not just as his housekeeper, but as his mistress. As his lover and friend.

The flyer in the mail had been the sign he needed. He'd given her over a year to cool off. He'd come to Florida, confident he could convince her.

But from the moment he'd walked into the charming, busy bakery, he'd started to have

doubts. As they went down the street, everyone they passed seemed to know her. Young
mothers pushing baby strollers, gray-haired
retired couples holding hands, children,
teenagers—they all greeted her with enthu-
siasm. Including—Rafael growled beneath
his breath—some men. Young men in their
twenties, carrying surfboards and scuba gear.
Older men with expensive wristwatches and
expensive cars. Young or old, every time one
of them smiled at Louisa, his eyes lingering
on her face and body, Rafael had to restrain
himself from punching a stranger.

As he and Louisa walked by Mallory
Square, Rafael set his jaw. He'd been so arrogant, so sure he could get his way on the
journey from Paris. But now, he looked down
at her from the corner of his eye. What did
he have to offer that would compete with the
vibrant life she'd created here for herself?

She had her own business, a life with her
sister and her niece, friends of her own. And
for all he knew, she had a lover. Or worse:
more than one…

"Key West," she began, "is the southern-
most settlement in the continental United
States…." She continued to describe the

island like a tour guide, but Rafael barely understood the words. He heard only the lovely sound of her beautiful voice. Only saw the movement of her lush pink lips. He couldn't look away from her as they walked down the sidewalk, then crossed the busy street.

"Are you hungry?" she asked suddenly.

He'd been openly staring at her, he realized. He forced himself to look away, to not look at her gorgeous face, her high cheekbones tanned by the sun. To not look at her sensual mouth, or the full shape of her breasts in her clingy blue tank top. To not notice how tiny her waist looked, barely the span of both his hands, above the wide sway of her hips and her impossibly long, tanned legs.

"Well?"

He swallowed, forcing himself to meet her eyes and only her eyes.

"I'm starving," he muttered.

"Come on, then," she said, giving him a brief, impersonal smile. "We can't let you leave on an empty stomach."

He followed her to a nearby food stand near Mallory Square. After placing her order, Louisa turned and thrust a piping hot fried pastry, wrapped in a napkin, into his hands.

"What's this?" he said, staring down at it.

"It's a conch fritter," she said, taking a bite of it. "Try it."

He tried not to watch the way her mouth moved as she chewed the greasy fried pastry. She licked a spot of grease from her lips, and he nearly shuddered.

Then he realized she was waiting expectantly. He reached for his wallet.

"No. My treat," she said brightly, stopping him. "You came all the way from Paris. It's the least I can do to feed you before you leave."

It was the second time she'd made the not-so-gentle hint about him leaving. But could he blame her, after the way he'd treated her? "Right." He cleared his throat. "Shall we go sit down?"

She shook her head. "I'd rather just walk as we eat."

"It's crowded." He felt the stares of passing tourists, and other people, locals who greeted Louisa by name with big smiles. Some of them were men. It irritated him to no end. He glanced at the wide vista of the beach. "How about we walk by the beach?"

"By the boardwalk? Sure. There's a path. Come on."

They walked in silence, the only sound the soft crunching of sand beneath their feet as they crossed the path. He felt the hot wind blow against his skin.

He looked at her out of the corner of his eye. He'd missed her. Dreamed about her. And now, seeing her like this, wearing almost nothing over her curvaceous body…

He wanted her.

So much he shook with it.

She ate with gusto, swiftly finishing her fritter. Lifting her eyebrows, she looked at his own fritter. He hadn't even taken a bite yet.

"Don't you like it?" she asked, her eyes glinting at him in the sunshine. She was daring him to say no. Taunting him to admit he only liked fancy gourmet food, the kind she'd prepared for him while she was his housekeeper in Paris.

She didn't know about all the years he'd barely existed in New York, where he'd started his commodities trading firm while still in college. He'd poured all his money into investments, barely surviving on the cheapest food he could get.

But he hadn't had to live that way for long. Success had come easily for him. He'd found that all it took to do well in the world was charm and confidence, and never, ever admitting when he had no clue what he was doing.

And the same was true of love affairs. No matter what women said, they did not want a man who was vulnerable. Kindness? They saw it as weakness. Whatever they said, women were attracted to one thing only: power.

Looking straight into her eyes, he took a bite of the conch fritter.

"It's good," he said. He took another bite, though he barely tasted the food. How could he explain that he had no appetite? He wanted only one thing.

He wanted Louisa in his bed.

"I'm sure it's not what you're used to," she said mockingly. "It's not exactly caviar and steak tartare."

He stuffed the rest of the fritter in his

mouth, not tasting it at all. He put the napkin in his coat pocket. He stopped halfway across the beach and looked at her.

Wind swirled her dark honey-colored hair around her face. Behind her, he could see the green leafy palm trees and brilliant bougainvillea. But the pink of the flowers was nothing compared to the roses in her cheeks, to the deep red of her lips.

He reached out to push back the dark blond tendrils of hair from her face. His fingertips brushed her warm skin. Touching her burned his fingertips.

She looked up at him, so close beneath the bright Florida sun, and he noticed for the first time that the eyes he'd always believed to be a regular brown were actually hazel, gleaming with a thousand tiny slivers of green and blue and brown like an explosion of light and color.

He took a deep breath.

"Come back to me, Louisa," he whispered.

She sucked in her breath, staring at him.

"I miss you." Reaching down, he took both of her hands in his own. Her fingers were slender and gentle and warm. He looked down at her intently. "I want you."

Their eyes locked. "You do?" she whispered. "Why?"

He couldn't tell her the full truth. Couldn't tell her how much he needed her. Right here. Right now. Being weak would never win him what he wanted; so he told her half the truth.

"My homes are in shambles," he said honestly. "The various housekeepers do their best, but no one organizes things like you. No one oversees things. I need a firm hand, I need your intelligent command. I need *you*."

She stared at him. Then she looked away, blinking fast. "You want me to work for you," she said dully. "That's what you need from me. You want me to be your housekeeper again."

"Yes." He paused. "I will quadruple your pay. Give you all the vacation time you need. Whatever you want."

Her lips curved. "You are generous," she whispered, but her tone was bitter. Then she turned to face him, her eyes suspiciously bright. "But I'm afraid I have no interest in being your housekeeper ever again."

Rafael clenched his hands into fists. From the moment he'd seen her in the bright bakery, looking so vibrant and happy as she served customers, it was just what he'd feared she would say.

But he couldn't accept that—couldn't!

"I told you I was sorry about what I said to you," he said quietly, "and I am. I over-reacted. Can't we put it all in the past?"

"It *is* in the past." She looked past him to the brightly colored booths across the road, to the single roving chicken squawking as it walked freely on the beach, flapping its wings. In the distance, children were laughing as they flew a kite in the breeze. Turning back to him, she gave a brief smile that didn't reach her eyes. "I'm not leaving Key West. I like it here. With my family…"

"I'll buy your sister an apartment near us in Paris."

"No, thank you."

Why was she being so stubborn? Was it truly because she loved this island so much—or was it because she'd already given her heart to another man? But he wouldn't think about that possibility, couldn't allow himself to think about it! He set his jaw. "I could offer you a great deal of money—"

"No!" She whirled on him fiercely. "We are *not* having a hard time with money. My little bakery is doing just fine, for your information. I don't want or need your help. I can support my own family. Without you." She gave him a hard look. "You'll have to find someone else to sort out your messy life." Her whole body seemed tight as she turned her back on him. "I need to get back to my bakery now."

"Louisa, wait!"

But she started walking away, so he had no choice but to hurry after her. His mind was spinning with ways to convince her to come back to him. But he could not think of anything he hadn't yet offered. They crossed back through the town where everyone seemed to know her, where everyone was glad to see her.

What could Rafael possibly offer her to compete with the life she'd created for herself?

"Here we are," she said briskly as they reached the door of her gingerbread-style shop beneath the overhanging awning on the wooden sidewalk. She held out her hand. "Goodbye."

Slowly he took her hand. But when he felt it in his own, he knew he could not let her go. He shook it, then instead of releasing her, pulled her hand closer, pulling her toward his body.

"Come back to me, Louisa," he said in a low voice. His eyes searched hers. "Not as my employee…but as my mistress."

Her jaw dropped. "What?"

"I've never tried to be faithful to one woman before," he said. "But since you left I haven't been able to forget you. I want to be with you, Louisa. Not as your boss. As your, your…lover." The word was pulled from him painfully. "I was a fool to let you go. A fool to push you away. You are the one woman who's never lied to me." He gave her a crooked smile. "The one woman who defied me when I deserved it, who dared to tell me when I was making an ass of myself. I need you."

She stared at him. "What are you saying?"

"I can't offer you marriage. But for as long

as we're together—" he took a deep breath "—I promise I will be faithful to you."

He heard her intake of breath, felt her tremble in his arms.

Suddenly an explosion of happiness went through him. *He knew he had convinced her.*

Lowering his mouth to hers, he gave her a long kiss full of passion and tenderness. He held her tightly, kissing her until he felt her surrender, until he felt her sigh in his arms. Until she started to kiss him back.

When he finally pulled away, he was smiling. He'd never been so happy.

"So you'll come?" he whispered, feeling more sure of himself now. Caressing her face, he smiled down at her. Louisa's eyelids fluttered open. She blinked in apparent bewilderment as he stroked her cheek and added, "My plane is waiting to take us to Buenos Aires."

She looked up at him. Then she sucked in her breath.

"No," she said. "Damn you! No!"

His jaw dropped as he stared at her, unable to believe her answer. He couldn't even fathom what he was hearing. For his whole

adult life, he'd been the legendary elusive
playboy. He'd never offered any woman as
much as he'd just offered Louisa.

So now to have her actually refuse him!

"Why?" he demanded over the lump in his
throat. He thought again of the men they'd
passed on the street who'd been so delighted
to see her. All those surfer boys looking at her
with longing, all those wealthy yacht-owners
who'd eyed her with lust. Rafael's expression
hardened. "Is there someone else?"

He heard her intake of breath as her eyes
flashed up at him.

"Yes," she said in a low voice. "There is
someone else. I'm sorry." She pulled her
hand out of his grasp, and he had the sudden
feeling of the warmth of her slipping away,
slipping away forever. "Goodbye," she whispered.

Turning in a whirl of vibrant color, she
pushed open the door into her bakery. He
heard the bright tinkle of the bell, and then
he was left alone on the wooden boardwalk,
beneath a cloudless sky stretching to the brilliant blue sea.

CHAPTER SEVEN

LOUISA's legs wobbled with emotion as she went back into the bakery.

She felt the sudden blast of warmth and light as she entered the shop, smelled bread baking in the oven, heard the laughter of her six-year-old niece talking to her baby son in his bouncy chair. She was home again, and safe. She'd kept her secret and left Rafael behind forever. She'd put her child first. He was the only one who mattered.

So why didn't she feel happier? Why did she feel so broken inside? She blinked her eyes fast, barely able to keep from crying, staring down at the floor.

The floor needed to be mopped, she thought dimly. She would do that first. And as her heart turned over in her chest she pushed away the memories of the man she'd tried for over a year to forget, the father of her baby. She tried to focus on her business, her child, the rest of her daily schedule. Anything but the man she'd just pushed away…

I can't offer you marriage. But for as long as we're together, I promise I will be faithful to you.

"Did you have a nice visit?" her sister said innocently as the last customer left carrying a box of caramel macadamia brownies. "I didn't expect you back for hours."

"Didn't you?" she said hoarsely.

"To be honest I'm glad to see you," Katie said with a sigh. "This is the first lull in traffic we've had since you left. A minute ago five people were waiting in line wanting cookies and tarts, and then the baby started to cry, and I thought I would lose my mind either laughing or crying…"

Louisa slowly lifted her head. Her eyes glittered at her sister.

"You sent that anonymous letter, didn't you? You brought him here."

Her voice was even, revealing nothing of her turmoil inside.

Katie stopped. Then she slowly nodded.

"Why?" Louisa said. She heard her baby

give a snuffling cry and walked swiftly behind the counter and lifted him from his bouncy seat, jiggling him on her hip as she continued to glare at her sister. "Why would you try to hurt me? Do you want him to take my son from me? Do you still hate me so much?"

"No!" her sister gasped, her expression horrified. Tears rushed into her eyes, the hazel-colored eyes so similar to Louisa's own, though her sister was several years younger and her hair was lightened into a luscious light blond color. She swallowed. "I once took away the man you loved. I am trying to make it up to you."

Louisa blinked at her in shock.

"I'm so sorry for what I did to you," Katie choked out. "I thought I loved Matthias. I thought you didn't. But I was wrong. So wrong to sleep with him. And I should have known. A man who would betray one person in his life would betray others…" Her voice trailed off bitterly. She looked up, openly weeping. "You've done so much for me. Always. I'll never forgive myself for taking Matthias away from you."

Matthias. The truth was that Louisa could

barely remember him now. How could she have ever thought she loved the man, when she'd barely known him?

Unlike Rafael, whom she knew so well in so many ways.

The way he played the piano at night when he was lonely, the way he would carelessly eat five of her caramel brownies before dinner. The way he loved the smell of roses in the springtime. The way he ate dinner at three in the morning, then rose for his coffee and newspaper three hours later. The way he ruthlessly cut people out of his life before they could disappoint him.

Louisa shook her head. "You were right all along. I never loved Matthias," she said in a low voice. Lifting her head, she gave a shuddering breath. "But Rafael..."

"You have to tell him," her sister said. "He has to know."

Louisa looked at Katie. "It's too late."

"It can't be," she whispered. "It can't be too late. I need to do something, something to make you forgive me...."

Six-year-old Madison, her blond hair in pigtails, reached her arms up anxiously around her weeping mother. "What's wrong, Mommy? Why are you crying?"

It had been almost two years since her father's death, and the little girl already had forgotten almost everything about her father.

"Nothing's wrong, sweetie," Katie said, wiping her eyes and trying to smile.

But so much was wrong, Louisa thought. She and Katie had had such a happy childhood in northern Florida, beloved and protected by both their parents. Then, all too young, their mother had died of a long, lingering illness, followed by their father six months later when he simply seemed to lose the will to live. They'd lost their parents. Her niece had lost her father. But that had been beyond their control.

Louisa was deliberately choosing to deprive her baby of his father, and though she tried to remind herself why she'd had no choice, suddenly pain ripped through her. She looked down at her baby. What if she'd made the wrong choice?

"Can you ever forgive me?" her sister whispered.

Reaching over, Louisa hugged Katie

fiercely with one arm. She realized she was crying, too. "There is nothing to forgive."

"I love you," Katie whispered. "And I want you to be happy. Do the right thing while you have the chance. Give your child a father."

"I can't tell him," Louisa said over the lump in her throat as she pulled away. "Rafael would be furious. He might try to take Noah away from me…."

"He wouldn't!"

"You didn't hear him last year when he said he would force me into marriage and make my life hell as his wife. If he ever knew I'd had his baby…"

She looked down at Noah. At almost eight months, he was a happy, chubby baby with fat legs and a smiley disposition. Other than his dark hair and the slate-gray color of his eyes, he was nothing like the man who'd fathered him.

"Whatever he said to you, he said in anger," Katie argued. "He wouldn't take Noah away from you. You're a good mother!"

"You don't understand," Louisa cried, wiping her tears away fiercely. "If Rafael knew I'd had his baby…*he would destroy me.*"

The words were still coming out of her mouth when Louisa heard the chiming bell of the door. She froze. Then, with her baby still against her hip, she turned.

Rafael stood in the doorway. He'd been reaching for the bag of caramel brownies that he'd left on the counter. But by the wide look in his eyes as he saw Louisa with the baby in her arms, she knew her worst fears had been realized. He knew everything.

"Rafael," she breathed. "I can explain."

He looked at the baby.

"Who is that?" he asked in a low voice.

"Rafael…he is…I wanted to…"

His eyes narrowed. His shoulders straightened, and his body seemed so tall and strong and powerful. His face was dark as he took a step toward her, and it took all of her courage to remain rooted in one spot.

"Is that baby mine?" His voice was cold. Dangerous.

The panicked thought raced through her brain that she should lie, say the baby was her sister's, or that she was babysitting for a neighbor—but as she looked up into his hard, gray eyes, her heart pounded in her throat. And she found she could not lie.

"Tell me." His voice was deceptively soft as he took another step toward her. "Who. Is. That. Baby."

Her teeth chattered. "He is…my son."

Coming very close to her, looking down at her without touching either her or Noah, he said in a voice low as a whisper and dark as night, "And who is the father?"

Lie! A voice inside her screamed. Lie!

But she could not. Even after everything she'd done, she could not look into his face and deny him the truth that was obvious. Everything about their son looked exactly like Rafael, from his black hair to his beautiful gray eyes.

"Is he my son?" Rafael said in a low voice.

Closing her eyes as if bracing for a blow, she took a deep breath.

"Yes," she whispered.

The simple, clipped word from her lips—*Yes*—nearly caused Rafael to stagger back, as if struck by a mortal blow. Even though he'd known the truth from the instant he saw the baby on Louisa's hip.

But hearing the word, beads of sweat broke

out over his forehead. His entire body felt like ice.

She'd had his baby. And she hadn't told him.

Louisa had caused him to unknowingly abandon his son.

His hands tightened as he stared at her across the warmth of the bakery. A large group of tourists entered the shop behind him with a happy chime of the bell.

With a snarl, Rafael opened his mouth to speak, to accuse. Grabbing his arm, still holding her baby against her hip, Louisa pulled Rafael up the flight of stairs behind the counter.

At the top of the stairs, he looked grimly at the second-floor apartment around him. It was a small, pretty, feminine home. Anxiously tugging on his arm, Louisa pulled him into a bedroom and closed the door behind him.

"Please understand," she said desperately, turning to face him. "You left me no choice!"

He stared around the small room. It contained a single bed, a crib and a changing table. The bed was covered by a handmade quilt. On the wall over the crib, soft fabric letters spelled out N-O-A-H beside a framed picture of a giraffe that looked like it was from an old children's book.

There was no lavish luxury here. This apartment wasn't a palace, but it was homey and cozy. It was bright and warm. The bedroom was decorated with warmth and simplicity—and kept absolutely clean.

Warmth. Love. Care. Everything Louisa had denied Rafael for the last year and a half. Along with the truth. *Along with his child.*

The rage of betrayal ripped through him.

"Rafael, please. Won't you talk to me?"

Slowly he turned back to stare at her. He'd thought Louisa Grey was different from any woman he'd known. He'd thought her an intelligent woman with a bright mind and a rare sense of dignity—of loyalty. In the years she'd worked for him, he'd looked forward to seeing her every night after he returned from a date. He'd become accustomed to seeing dark eyes gleam through her glasses as she made him a late-night turkey-and-baguette and listened with some amusement to his latest dating woes, which always involved some woman going to pieces after he dumped her.

"It's your own fault, you know," she'd chided him gently. "You treat them badly."

"I make them no promises," he'd protested. "I tell them our affair cannot last. I am not a man made for marriage."

"You might tell them that, but your eyes say something else," she'd said quietly. "I've seen you. You look at every woman as if she, and only she, might be the one to make you faithful."

Rafael exhaled. She'd been right, of course. Louisa saw through all of his lies—even the ones he hadn't realized he was telling. She'd made herself indispensable in his life. Unique.

And now this. Her vengeful cruelty took his breath away.

Had Louisa Grey always been a liar? Or had Rafael turned her into a liar—when he'd slept with her?

No! He wasn't going to think that way— wasn't going to give her any excuse to say he was the one at fault for her crime. He wasn't the one who'd done this! All these months, he'd felt so guilty, thinking he'd treated her badly. And all along, she was the one who'd lied to him. *She'd stolen his child.*

If not for the anonymous letter, he might never have come here. His baby might always have grown up believing Rafael had abandoned him.

His hands clenched into fists. He'd once thought Louisa a gold digger. Now he wished she were. A gold digger would have at least contacted him for a payout. This was far worse. Louisa Grey was a vindictive, cold, ruthless woman.

Rafael looked at the child in her arms. What kind of woman could keep a baby a secret from his own father?

"What is his name?" he said harshly.

She looked at him with pleading eyes. "You told me you never wanted a child, Rafael. You said—"

"That's your excuse?" he bit out furiously. "You use my own words against me? I also told you that if you were pregnant, I would marry you."

"But I didn't want to marry you!"

He stared at her, then shook his head in fury. "No, you didn't, did you?" he said. "You wanted revenge for the way I treated you. And you knew this would hurt me as nothing else ever could."

"That's not true!" she gasped. "You made it clear you never wanted a wife or child! Do you think I would share my precious baby with a man who didn't even want him?"

He narrowed his eyes. "It wasn't your decision to make."

She took a deep breath, shifting position from her left leg to the right as the baby squirmed in her arms.

Without warning, Rafael took the baby away from her. He saw Louisa choke back a protest, saw her clench her hands at her sides, as if fighting her initial instinctive reaction to snatch the baby back into her own arms.

He looked down at the baby. "My son," he whispered. "You are my son."

"His name is Noah, after my father," she said unwillingly behind him. "Noah Grey."

Holding the baby tenderly, he whirled to face her in a swift and decisive motion. "Noah *Grey?* You did not even give him my name?"

She shook her head stubbornly.

"You lied to me, Louisa," he said softly. He looked from his precious young son to the lying woman who had given birth to him. He saw her tremble, but kept himself from touching her—from raging at her, from shaking her—by an act of fierce will. "You are a far greater liar than I ever imagined." He gave a low, harsh laugh. "And to think you said you *loved* me," he sneered. "That's what your love was worth!"

Her cheeks went hot. "I did love you," she said quietly. "It nearly killed me."

He narrowed his eyes at her. "So that is why you lied to me about being on birth control? Because you thought you were in love with me?"

"I didn't lie!"

"Then how did you get pregnant?"

"I was on the Pill in Paris, like I told you," she whispered, then shook her head. "The whole staff ate some bad fish from the market. I threw up for days. I never thought that it might make the Pill useless, but then," her cheeks colored, "I never paid much attention to the birth control aspects of the medication. I never expected you to seduce me!"

Silence fell. Through the sheer curtains at the large sash window, with its brightly painted open shutters, he could see clouds trailing across the blue sky, above the distant turquoise sea. He took a deep breath.

"Perhaps you're not lying," he said quietly. "For if you were truly a gold digger, you would have jumped at the chance to marry me. The pregnancy must have been an accident." He set his jaw as he looked down at his son. "But your lie to me for the last year and a half was not."

"You're not being fair!" she cried. "You told me you never wanted a child. If I'd told you I was pregnant, you'd have insisted I was a gold digger who'd purposefully set out to 'trap' you!"

"Like the devil, you twist my own words against me," he said, then gave a low laugh. "You are the most cold, heartless woman I have ever known. Which is a high mark indeed."

"I'm not," she whispered.

"You looked into my face and lied to me. *I'm not pregnant,* you said." He nearly choked on the words. "When were you planning to tell me the truth, Louisa? After he was a grown man? Or did you mean to punish our son as well as me," he said harshly, "by only telling him the truth after I was dead?"

She went pale. "I would never do that to you."

"You already have."

Pain racked his body. Louisa had hurt him in the most devastating way possible.

And when he thought of how, just a half hour ago, they'd walked along the beach, he'd humbly held his heart in his hands and asked her to be his lover...

He shuddered with humiliation and fury. Then, still holding the baby, he turned without a word.

"Where are you going?"

"I'm taking my son home."

"No!" she shrieked. Racing ahead of them, she blocked the door. "You can't take my baby away from me—you can't!"

"We'll come to a custody arrangement." He had the satisfaction of seeing her shoulders sag with relief before he mercilessly continued, "You've had Noah for the last eight months. I will take him for the next eight months." Cradling his baby son against his shirt, he turned to go. "You will hear from my lawyers sometime before next Christmas."

"No!" she screamed, pulling on his arm. "You can't take him from me—his mother! Not for eight months!"

He glanced back at her coldly. "Can I not? But that is what you have done to me. You've had your time. I will have mine. Is that not 'fair' enough for you?" he said mockingly.

"No," she wept freely. "Please. It would kill me."

Rafael looked down at her. Somehow, in her abject grief and surrender, even with her nose red and tears streaking down her cheeks, she was still beautiful. He still wanted her. It infuriated him.

He heard the baby start to cry, his loud wailing mingling with Louisa's. Rafael awkwardly tried to comfort the baby, but could not. He had no experience with babies and no idea how to comfort Noah. He did not know his own son. The injustice of it raged in his heart as, setting his jaw, he gently handed the baby to Louisa.

"Noah. Oh, Noah." Louisa's weeping only intensified as she cradled her baby against her, whispering words of love, kissing his chubby cheeks again and again. "Oh, my sweet baby."

Rafael stared down at them. He took a deep breath. And came to a sudden decision.

"*Vale,*" he said through clenched teeth. "I will not separate you."

"Thank you," Louisa whispered.

He stared at her coldly. "It's for my son's sake. Not yours."

She rocked the baby in her arms, her breath still uneven between sobs and hiccups. Rafael looked at her, then looked slowly around the room, from the sheer curtains over the window to the giraffe on the wall above the crib.

She was, he thought grudgingly, a decent mother. What she would not be—what she could never be again—was a woman he could trust.

But that didn't stop Rafael from wanting her.

There is someone else, she'd said.

Who was the man? Rafael's hands clenched. How many lovers had been in Louisa's bed over the last year, while he'd tossed and turned, tormented by longing for his fantasy of her as he'd believed her to be— honest, loving, chaste?

For all these years, Louisa Grey was the

one woman he'd never been able to completely possess.

Now, he wanted to punish her. To break down her elusiveness. To own her.

Then discard her like the rest.

An idea occurred to him. A cruel, perfect idea.

It would be a neat, tidy, perfect revenge.

He smiled grimly. Walking across the nursery, he placed his hand on her shoulder.

"There is just one condition," he said brutally.

"Anything," she whispered. "Just don't separate me from my son."

Lowering his head, Rafael gave her a seductive kiss. He possessed her mouth with his, luring her with his tongue. He felt her shiver in his arms. He felt her sigh, then surrender.

When he pulled away, he saw the haze of longing in her eyes, and hid a smile.

She thought she'd beaten him, but he would make her pay. He was the master of the cold-hearted seduction. Soon, his possession of her would be complete.

"You will be completely mine," he whispered. He stroked her cheek as he looked down at her, his eyes glittering in the shadowy room. "You will marry me, Louisa."

CHAPTER EIGHT

"WELCOME to Buenos Aires, Señora Cruz."

As the doorman greeted her, Louisa barely had time to wonder how he already knew about the marriage before bodyguards hustled her inside the *Belle Époque* high-rise in the exclusive Recoleta district. In two seconds, they'd crossed the lavish marble floor and were in the elevator.

Tall, hulking men clustered all around her, making Louisa feel small as she cradled her baby nervously in her arms. Worst of all: the tallest and most powerful of the men around her was Rafael. *Her new husband.*

When she'd woken up in Key West that morning, Louisa had never imagined she could find herself taken to Buenos Aires as the wife of a man who hated her. He kissed her so well that she almost imagined, in his arms, that he could forgive her. But when he pulled away from her, he could not hide the coldness in his slate eyes.

Within minutes after he'd demanded marriage, he'd dragged her to the courthouse. He'd somehow managed to convince the clerk Louisa was not a Florida resident and to skip the three-day waiting period. Before they'd even left Key West, Louisa had been his lawfully married wife. He'd spent the long flight on his private jet working. Ignoring her.

Now, in the elevator, Rafael's dark eyes gleamed at her malevolently. What did he intend to do to her?

I would make you pay for trapping me into marriage. I would make you pay...and pay... and pay.

At least she still had her baby in her arms, she comforted herself. That was what mattered. When she'd thought Rafael meant to take their son away, she'd been so frightened, she'd known she would do anything— *anything*—to stay with Noah. And so she'd said farewell to her sister and niece, telling her she was eloping with Rafael.

Katie had been ecstatic for her. "We'll be

fine with the bakery until you get back," she'd said joyfully. "Have a wonderful time!"

If only her sister knew the truth. Louisa feared she was never going back to that warm, loving home in Key West. Rafael would never let her go.

When the elevator reached the top floor, Rafael pushed open the double doors.

"Welcome home," he said sardonically.

"Home?" Louisa looked around her in dismay. The old luxury apartment was old, musty and desperately in need of cleaning and refurbishment. All the furniture was covered with white sheets, which gave it a ghostly appearance. But in spite of her anger and fear, she could not help but observe the space with a professional eye and see the loveliness beneath the neglect. It had high Edwardian plaster ceilings and a view of the city through wide windows. Against her will, she could almost see how to make this apartment beautiful again. How to make it a home.

"I had no idea it was in such disarray," she whispered.

He shrugged. "I'm not here often."

She looked at him out of the corner of her eye. "I could make it nice," she offered.

"Don't bother," he said shortly. "We won't be here for long."

Louisa shivered. Now that she was his bride, now that they shared a child, he had more power over her than ever before. After five years of obeying his orders as his housekeeper, it would have been easy to return to the habit of trying to please him. But her time living in Key West had changed her. She had finally found her voice.

"This house could be so lovely," she said softly.

His lips twisted. "Do not fall in love. We will be here only a few days." He pushed open a door. "You will sleep in here."

This bedroom, at least, had been neatly tended. A small crib had been set up in the darkest corner near the large, modern bed.

With an intake of breath, Louisa turned back to him, her eyes shining. She'd wondered if he had any goodness left in his soul, but he must. Or why else would he have been so kind? "Thank you for letting me sleep in the same room as the baby. I promise you can trust me. I won't take Noah anywhere without your permission."

"I know you won't." His eyes were dark. "Because you and I will be sharing a bed."

She looked sharply at the bed. The enormous bed. And imagined what he planned to do to her there.

She'd thought she would do anything to keep her baby...but this?

Give her body to the man who hated her? Who had such power over her? Who wanted revenge for the way she'd kept his son a secret?

She repressed a shiver, remembering the last time they'd been in bed together on the private Greek island. She'd been so happy then. He'd made her light up with joy from without and within, given her such pleasure she hadn't even imagined it possible.

If she gave him her body ever again, how much longer would it be before he owned every inch of her soul?

Any woman who loved Rafael Cruz would ultimately be destroyed by that love. Because he had no love to give. He offered only seduction, not love. He had a heart of ice.

And if at times he seemed to care, if he

seemed to be vulnerable after all, that was the most dangerous illusion of all.

Straightening her shoulders, she turned to face him. "I won't sleep with you."

"You will," he said, a sensual smile tracing his mouth. "You are my wife."

She licked her lips. "Just because we are legally married does not mean you own me!"

"Does it not?" he said softly.

He approached her, and for a moment she thought he intended to kiss her. Then the baby started to whimper and squirm in her arms. He stopped.

"Take care of my son," he said. "When you are done, I will be waiting."

Cuddling Noah in the bedroom, she fed him once they were alone. When he was asleep, she tucked him tenderly into the crib. The only sound was the quiet, even breathing of their sleeping baby as she finally left the bedroom, closing the door softly behind her.

She looked up with an intake of breath when she saw him waiting for her at the end of the hall, a dark, towering figure in a house full of shadows.

Rafael's eyes never left hers as he came slowly toward her. He put his hands on her shoulders, and she shivered.

How long could she resist him?

God help her if he ever reverted to the charming, seductive man she'd once known, the man with a gift for words and a light in his dark eyes that could convince any woman that she, and only she, could bring out the good in his heart.

God help her if Rafael decided to make her love him again.

"Come," he whispered.

Taking her hand, he pulled her down the hall. Dinner had been catered in and served on the massive oak dining table overlooking the wall of windows and the view of the city. The servers set up the food, then departed, along with the bodyguards.

Louisa was alone with Rafael, with no chaperone but their sleeping baby down the hall. She looked out toward the windows, past the ghostly white furniture covered with sheets. He opened a bottle of Argentinian red wine and poured it into two crystal goblets.

It should have felt intimate, and yet in the neglected penthouse it felt cold. Soulless. The food was delicious, but this place didn't feel like home. It felt dead. It felt like a prison.

And Rafael was her jailer.

She thought of the snug little apartment she'd left behind in Key West, of the sunshine and sound of the sea and her niece's laughter, and felt a lump in her throat. She set down her fork with a clang against the china plate.

"Don't you like the *empanadas?*" he asked.

"They're delicious," she murmured. "But it doesn't feel like home."

"Still a housekeeper at heart?" he said mockingly.

She lifted her chin. "I'd rather cook for us. For our family."

"Just take care of Noah. That is enough. We won't be here long." His eyes narrowed, and the darkness in his gaze scared her. "I have some business in Buenos Aires. A payback that has been a long time coming." He smiled. "Once that's done, *querida,*" he said, "we will return to Paris."

Paris. She thought of her memories there with a shiver. Back to Paris. Where she'd first surrendered to her desire for her playboy boss. Where she thought he'd opened up his soul to her.

She couldn't let herself fall for him again—couldn't!

He might have some kind of sensual power over her that she could not fight—but she wouldn't let him have her soul!

She took a deep breath, squaring her shoulders.

"I cannot just live with you, doing nothing," she said quietly. "I married you and came to Buenos Aires because you left me no choice, but you must see that this cannot last. Let me at least act the part of your housekeeper. Because you do not want me as your wife."

"And you?" he said mockingly. "Do you want me as your husband?"

She swallowed, trying not to remember the ridiculous dreams she'd had after she'd first found out she was pregnant, when she'd dreamed of Rafael falling in love with her. When she'd imagined him changing somehow into a good father, a good husband. Then, she'd wanted...

She shook her head. She wouldn't think

of it! "I was doing fine on my own. Noah and I were happy in Key West."

"Too bad." He took a drink of the expensive red wine from the crystal glass. "You're never going back."

It was exactly what she'd feared he would say, but she lifted her head defiantly. "Of course we're going back. I have a business to run, and a family that needs me—"

"Consider the bakery a gift to your sister," he said carelessly. "She now owns it."

She stared at him in shock, then narrowed her eyes.

"You are *out of your mind*," she said tersely, stabbing her fork toward him in midair for emphasis, "if you think I'll let you just give away the business I love, the business I built and created with my life savings after I worked for you for *five hard years*—"

"Yes, I am certain that was a fate worse than death," he said coolly, taking another sip of the red wine. "But your sister and her daughter will do well with the bakery. They will be happy and secure. That is what you want, is it not?"

She ground her teeth.

"Of course it is. But I want to be there

with them! I've missed too much time with them already," she said softly, then shook her head. "Florida is my home. You cannot take me away from a place where I've made friends—"

"*Sí,*" he said sardonically. "I saw your many *friends* when I was there. Why don't you admit the truth about why you're so desperate to return?"

"Because I hate the sight of you?"

To her frustration, he seemed untouched by her jab. He only gave her a cold smile. "Who is he?"

"He?"

"The man you have been seeing. Or was there more than one? I might have been your first experience in bed, but how long did you wait for your second and third and fourth?" His cold eyes met hers over the table. "Tell me, Louisa. How many men did you invite to your bed while you were still pregnant with my child?"

She stared at him in horror. Then, she rose from the table. Looking down at him, she raised her hand but he grabbed her wrists. He was so strong she could not pull away.

He stared at her for a moment in cold fury.

She felt the pounding of her own heart, heard the soft gasp of her own breath. Felt the electricity in the air suddenly change between them.

Then, lowering his head to hers, he claimed her mouth in a punishing kiss.

Louisa tried to fight. Tried to push him away. He was bruising her, hurting her—

Then his kiss suddenly gentled. His hold on her became seductive, his arms caressing her softly, so softly, that her shirt and shorts disappeared as if blown off her body by a light warm breeze. His lips moved against her so tenderly, so lovingly, that she could not resist.

She wrapped her arms around his neck as he lifted her up into his arms and carried her, not to the bed, but to the nearby couch covered with a white sheet. There, he made love to her with such amazing tenderness that she wept.

Afterward, as she held him and he slept in her arms, she looked out at the view of the city and was suddenly reminded of their first night together, in Paris. The night she'd admitted to herself that she was in love with him.

Now, she looked at him in the slanted light from the windows, curled up beside her on the long, wide sofa covered with the white sheet. She listened to the rise and fall of his breath, felt the warmth of his skin against her cheek, heard the beat of his heart with her head against his chest.

And knew she still loved him.

She'd been in love with him secretly, hopefully, desperately for years. The sixteen months they'd spent apart, where she'd tried to convince herself she didn't love him anymore, had changed nothing.

She loved him.

And, from the way he'd touched her in the night, was it possible he could love her…?

No, she told herself fiercely. *It's just his nature. His body promises what his soul cannot deliver.*

And yet…

They had a child together. Could somehow, by some miracle, Louisa be the one to reach Rafael's heart, to make him whole, to heal his soul so they could be the real, loving family she longed for them to be?

She heard Noah cry. Quietly, so she wouldn't wake her husband, she crept out of his arms and went down the hall. Pulling on her clothes, she padded softly across the apartment to feed the baby and rock him back to sleep.

She returned to the living room with her heart in her throat, full of dreams and plans and hopes to help Rafael be the man she needed. The man she loved. The man she was convinced he was born to be. She could hardly wait to sleep in his arms....

She stopped abruptly when she saw the sofa was empty.

He came up behind her. She whirled around to discover him wearing a white terry cloth robe, clearly just come from the shower.

"That was enjoyable," he said coolly, drying his wet hair with a towel. "I think I may like having a wife."

She tilted her head, her heart pounding with hope. "You think so?" she whispered.

His lips curved. "Of course. You're in my bed. At my service. And apparently wishing to cook and clean for me whenever you're not satisfying me in bed. I'm saving a great deal of money, since I don't even have to pay you. You are—" he reached out to stroke her cheek "—every man's dream wife."

She swallowed, trembling as she looked up into his cold gray eyes. "You are trying to hurt me. Why?"

"I said I will enjoy our marriage. And you—will not." Pulling his hand away, he leaned forward until his handsome face was inches from her own. "Nothing has changed," he whispered. His eyes were a mesmerizing gray. "You will regret the day you stole my son away from me."

Pain stabbed through her. Was that all their night together had been for him? She'd thought—dreamed—it could be some kind of new start for them, the sweet promise of forgiveness and a new life, raising their son together.

He'd fooled her yet again. His tenderness, his sensuality, had been the weapons he'd used to punish her!

She had the sudden image of the pain he could inflict on her, this man she loved, this man she'd once known so well.

I can't offer you marriage. But for as long as we're together, I promise I will be faithful to you.

She sucked in her breath. He'd cared for her. He still did. It was only his anger that was making him try to hurt her!

But she wouldn't let him. She wouldn't let him destroy their chance of being a family. Somehow, in spite of everything, she would break through his anger and make him forgive her!

It was their only hope....

She looked up at him. She could tell he was waiting for her to get upset, to yell, to cry.

Instead she took a deep breath. "I'm sorry."

"Sorry?" he ground out. "For stealing my son? You think an apology is enough?"

She nodded. "I thought I had no choice," she said simply. "If I'd told you I was pregnant in Istanbul, you would have insisted I was a gold digger—and punished me. Instead I tried to raise our son on my own, without any help from you. So you accuse me of being vindictive—and you want to punish me." She lifted her eyes to meet his. "Have you ever considered that you are an impossible man to please? Have you ever considered," she said quietly, "that the problem might be *you?*"

He stared at her.

"Are you joking?" he growled.

She folded her arms over the paper-thin fabric of her tank top, wishing she had more clothes than her little shirt and shorts, more armor to protect her as she faced him. If only, she thought, she had one of her old gray woolen suits, her old thick black-framed glasses!

But all she had was herself. That would have to be enough.

She took a deep breath. "I still love you, Rafael," she whispered, then gave him a tremulous smile. "There. I said it. In spite of your faults, in spite of your weakness, I love you."

"My weakness?" he exploded.

She shivered at the danger in his dark eyes. But she still forced herself to be brave enough to speak the truth in her heart.

"A strong man," she said, "allows himself to be vulnerable. He shows his love at any cost. A truly strong man gives everything he has—everything he is—to his family. He loves with all his heart and holds nothing back!"

"And where did you learn that? House-keeping school?" he sneered.

"No," she said simply, facing down his sarcasm. "I learned it from my father, who though he never made a fortune, he made us feel every day like we were valued and loved."

Rafael sucked in his breath through his teeth.

"Forget it," he barked. Pulling on some jeans and a black T-shirt, he stuffed his feet into black Italian-made shoes and headed for the door.

"Where are you going?"

He looked back at her just once. His face was dark in the shadows of the apartment.

"Out," he said.

"Out? Out where? It's midnight!"

He gave a hard laugh. "The night is young—for me. I guess I'm too *weak* to stay." His eyebrows lowered as he ordered her, "Be ready for me upon my return. Perhaps I will want you again." A cold smile curved his mouth. "Perhaps not."

She stared at him, her heart throbbing painfully in her throat.

"Don't do this, Rafael," she choked out,

blinking back tears. "Stay and talk to me. Please. I want so much for us to—"

"I've had enough *talk* for one night," he said coldly. Opening the door, he walked out. She saw him have a quiet word with the huge bodyguard outside as the door closed behind him.

Louisa shook with humiliation and despair. She went to the window and stepped out onto the wrought-iron balcony, staring out into the twinkling lights of Recoleta and all Buenos Aires beyond it in the warm, humid night.

Looking down, she watched Rafael leave the building, watched him with her heart in her throat and tears streaking her face.

He glanced up. Their eyes met.

Then he coldly turned away. He climbed into the yellow sports car his bodyguard had brought to the curb. Stepping on the gas, he drove off into the night.

Where was he going? Louisa wondered with anguish. To meet another woman?

She stayed on the balcony for a long time after he left, feeling trapped, feeling helpless. The city at her feet still seemed to be busy and alive, noisy and young. All of the things she no longer felt.

Louisa was so tired, but she knew she would not be able to sleep. Not when her emotions were so wound up. Not when pain and love and helplessness made her shake.

Then she had an idea.

If Rafael couldn't stand a direct discussion, she would come at him sideways.

She would lure him into their marriage through the weak point he would never think to guard. She would seduce him with her skills. She would give him a home.

A small smile traced her lips as she left the balcony. Crossing the apartment, she flung open the front door. She spoke directly to his head bodyguard outside, an American named Evan Jones who rose respectfully to his feet.

"I need your help," she told him coolly, in her housekeeper voice that no staff member could ever resist. And neither did he.

As she gave him her instructions, Louisa suddenly felt a surge of optimism. She might no longer be Rafael's housekeeper, but she still had power in his life. More than she'd ever had before. And though he did not know it, Rafael himself had given it to her. He'd done it when he'd made her his wife.

CHAPTER NINE

RAFAEL didn't return to the apartment until noon the next day.

He'd met some old school friends for a drink, but when women had come up to them at the bar, he'd found himself bored. Not just bored—uncomfortable. And so he'd left.

But he couldn't go home. Not after what Louisa had said.

In spite of your faults, in spite of your weakness, I love you.

His hands clenched to remember it. How did she dare? His weakness? No woman had ever said such a thing to him before! He'd intended to punish her, and yet somehow she'd gotten one step ahead of him!

His weakness.

Louisa knew him too well. She'd lived with him, day in and day out, for five years. No other woman had had such an opportunity to see beneath the facade. Or so thoroughly get under his skin. *She knew him.*

Rafael didn't like it. It made him feel weak, like she claimed him to be. And so he'd checked into the Four Seasons hotel to teach her a lesson; to prove to them both who was in control, and how easily he could hurt her. Let her suffer the same suspicions he himself had suffered in Key West with her. Let Louisa wonder what other lovers might be taking her place!

He had her ring on his finger. And as long as he did, he would never cheat on her. His honor would not allow it. As long as he was with her, he would be faithful.

But she didn't have to know that. She already had too much power over him.

A strong man allows himself to be vulnerable. He shows his love at any cost. A truly strong man gives everything he has—everything he is—to his family. He loves with all his heart and holds nothing back…! Have you ever considered that you are an impossible man to please? Have you ever considered that the problem might be you?

He was the problem? Him?

Rafael growled to himself in the elevator. She was the one who'd stolen his son!

Ignoring his bodyguard's cheerful greeting, Rafael pushed open his front door. And froze in the doorway.

For a moment, he thought he'd wandered into the wrong house. This surely could not be his apartment. It did not look remotely like the same place!

The old apartment had been thoroughly scrubbed, and all the old dusty knickknacks had been swept away along with the ghostly white covers. Fresh flowers were on the kitchen table. He could smell something delicious baking in the oven.

And how the hell had she managed to replace the old, heavy-set wooden furniture with new modern sofas, sleek chairs and a huge big-screen TV—all in the space of just a few hours?

"Welcome home, Rafael," he heard Louisa say behind him warmly, and he whirled to face her.

His wife looked incredibly pretty, smiling up at him, wearing a sweet, demure dress. He was immediately attracted in spite of himself. Taking a deep breath, he looked away—only to have his eyes fall upon the platter of caramel macadamia brownies cooling on the counter.

Louisa Grey—Louisa Cruz—was indeed everything any man would want. Sexy, strong, smart as hell. A good mother and a good cook. She was everything he'd ever wanted.

Except he hated her. Didn't he?

"How did you do all this?"

"I have my ways." She smiled mischievously, and love shone in her eyes. "I made the house a home. For us. For our family."

"I see," he said faintly.

He'd come home expecting a scene. He'd expected Louisa to scream and yell at him and wail, as other women had done when he'd pushed them away. Staying out all night was the swiftest, most convenient way he'd found to end a relationship.

But Louisa didn't even ask him where he'd been all night. It was as if she weren't even worried, as if she had complete confidence that she was the only woman he wanted.

And it was true, damn her.

She had too much control over him by

half. She knew him too well. And he couldn't simply end their relationship and walk away, no matter how much easier that seemed. They were married. They had a child.

But Rafael knew what she wanted. She wanted his soul. No matter how beautiful she was. No matter how tempting. He wouldn't give it to her. He would never let himself be vulnerable again.

He took a deep breath, keeping his expression cold.

"I did not give you permission to do this," he said. "I liked the house left how it was. I told you."

"Well, I didn't like it."

"It's not for you to choose—"

"It wasn't a healthy environment for the baby." She held out the platter. "Brownie?"

Caramel macadamia nut with white chocolate chips. His favorite. He narrowed his eyes. Did she truly think him so weak that he could be bought so simply?

"I'm not hungry."

She shrugged, then cut herself a big piece. Her smile spread into a joyful grin. He watched her bite into the gooey caramel brownie, with its layers of butterscotch and macadamia nut. Melted white chocolate smudged her lip. He watched her lick it off. His mouth watered.

But it wasn't the brownie he wanted anymore. He hungered for Louisa.

Her body.

Her laugh.

All of her.

Making love to her last night had been incredible. He'd seduced her to punish her but in the end, he was the one who'd been caught. He'd woken up, bereft of her in his arms. He hadn't liked the feeling. He'd jumped in the shower. He'd tried to pretend to them both that finally having her in his arms again, finally making love to her after sixteen months of yearning, had meant nothing.

But he could not lie to himself. Not anymore.

Rafael watched her pick up the baby from his bouncy seat and lift him on her hip. As she sang songs to Noah, swinging him in her arms as they twirled around the kitchen, her eyes danced with laughter.

He watched Louisa laughing with the baby in her arms. He looked at them, his heart in his throat.

He'd married her yesterday intending to discard her in Paris. Now, he realized his plans had changed. Louisa brought so much to his life. Why should he ever let her go?

He could still get the revenge he'd planned. Then he could take Louisa to Paris and they could start a new life....

"By the way," he said abruptly, "my mother is coming for dinner tonight."

Louisa stopped, clearly startled. Then her eyes lit up. "Your mother? How lovely!" she exclaimed. She tickled the baby, making him squeal with laughter as she cooed, "And she'll get to meet her sweet new grandbaby, won't she?"

Yes, she would. For the first and last time.

Grabbing the knife, Rafael cut himself an enormous piece of brownie. He took a huge bite. It was delicious. Like the taste of vengeance.

Louisa beamed up at him as he ate. He could see that she thought he was starting to bend, to break, beneath her influence. Well, let her continue to think so.

He smiled at her.

She would soon learn the truth. Rafael

would neither bend, nor break, for any woman. He would be the last one standing.

He'd once begged Louisa to remain his housekeeper. He'd once pleaded with her to become his mistress.

Marrying her had changed everything.

The marriage license would hold her as no employment contract ever could. Louisa would warm his bed, take care of his child and prepare his meals. The fact that she was now his wife meant he would never have to pay her. He'd never have to give her a vacation. And he'd never have to fear losing her again.

She was his wife. He owned her now. Forever.

"Welcome, *Mamá*."

Louisa watched Rafael kiss the stooped woman on both cheeks as he welcomed his mother to their home. Agustina Cruz was nothing like Louisa had expected. She'd thought Rafael's mother would be a slender, severely elegant socialite. Instead she was plump, gray-haired and had a timid, hopeful smile on her bright coral lips as she looked at her tall, handsome son.

"Buenas noches, mi hijo," she said to Rafael. "I am so happy to see you," she said in Spanish, standing on her tiptoes to embrace him. Louisa's high school Spanish was rusty after so many years in France, but she could still understand as Agustina continued tearfully, "It has been too long. I haven't heard from you since I sent you the letter after your father died."

"I remember," Rafael said coolly in English. "Come in."

Why was he being so strangely cold? Louisa thought. This woman was his mother! Whoever his father had been—she was the one who'd given birth to him, loved him, raised him!

She'd hoped that Rafael was starting to forgive her, that he was starting to allow the goodness of his heart to shine through. But now…she didn't know what to think.

Holding her own baby against her hip, Louisa smiled at the older woman.

"Welcome to our home, Señora Cruz," she added warmly in English. "I am so happy to meet you at last."

The other woman blinked at Louisa in her white cotton tea-length dress, peering at baby

Noah in a white shirt and black pants with a little tie. Louisa had chosen their clothes with care. Meeting Rafael's mother was important to her. And yet—she glanced over at Rafael. He was casually dressed in a black shirt and dark jeans. Why had he, alone in the group, made no effort?

Agustina blinked at Louisa and the baby. "Thank you, my dear. But who are you?"

"I am Rafael's new wife."

Agustina turned reproachful eyes upon her son, still standing grim and silent behind them. "Rafael, you are married?" she chided gently.

He shrugged.

"And this," Louisa added quickly, to cover up for her husband's coldness, "is our baby. Noah."

Agustina stared at the baby. "Your...your baby?" she gasped. Tears filled her eyes. "My grandson?"

Louisa nodded. Smiling, she placed the baby in his grandmother's arms.

"Oh *mi nieto, mi pequeño angelito,*" the woman whispered. Tears fell unheeded down her face as she held the baby in her arms.

Watching her joy, tears filled Louisa's eyes

as well. She looked back at her husband with a smile, expecting to see the same emotion in his face. Instead his dark eyes were blank. Expressionless. *Dead.*

"Come," he said in a low voice. "Let's sit down for dinner."

The meal was a joyful one—at least for the baby, mother and grandmother. Agustina Cruz was a lovely, warm, charming woman. She reminded Louisa of her own mother, whom she missed very much.

"That was delicious," Agustina said at the end of the meal, when she'd finished the last bite of Louisa's brownies covered with vanilla ice cream and butterscotch crumble.

"Thank you." Louisa had insisted on preparing the meal herself, as an expression of respect and care. Rafael had scoffed at that idea, then shrugged and let her do it.

Louisa had thought, when he'd come home at noon after being out all night, that she'd done everything she could to make him happy here. She'd worked on the house most of the night and all of the morning between caring for the baby. She'd dressed with care. She'd baked his favorite foods. She'd really thought she was starting to get through to him...especially after she'd been able to learn from the bodyguard, to her intense relief, that Rafael had spent the previous night alone at a hotel.

It had killed her to pretend she didn't care. But she knew Rafael too well. She couldn't play by the same rules as his other women had done. She had to keep him guessing. Keep him off balance. It was her only hope of gaining what she truly wanted.

His happiness—and her own.

Agustina set down her fork. "What an amazing meal."

"Louisa made it. To honor you," Rafael said coldly.

Gratitude and joy washed over his mother's face.

"Thank you. Both of you," Agustina said tearfully. "I was so afraid you'd never forgive me, Rafael. You must believe that I never meant to hurt you when I wouldn't share your father's name...."

"Hate you? Why would I hate you?" He took another drink of brandy then set the empty glass hard against the table. "Just because you waited until he was dead—just because you made sure I never had a real father and left me begging you for answers for twenty years—why would I hate you?"

Her plump cheeks had gone pale. "Rafael," she whispered, "I thought you understood."

"I do understand. And now—" he rose to his feet "—you will finally understand as well. You will know how it feels." He stared down at her. "You've met my family. For the first and only time. Now, you will never see them again."

"What?" Louisa gasped.

He picked up Noah. "We are never coming back to Buenos Aires. My son—" he looked down at the happy, smiling baby "—will never remember he has a grandmother. He will never even know you exist. You will die as my father died," he said harshly. "Alone."

His mother looked as if she might faint.

"Rafael—you cannot do this," Louisa gasped, pushing herself to her feet. "I won't let you do this!"

"It's your choice," he said evenly. He gave her a hard look. "Choose my mother, a stranger to you—or choose your husband and child."

Still holding the baby in his arms, he left the room.

Louisa started to run after them, then abruptly stopped. She looked down at Agustina, who was still sitting at the table, alone and forlorn.

"I'm sorry," Louisa choked out. "I will try to talk to him!"

The older woman looked at her, then sadly and steadily shook her head. "It will do no good, my dear," she said softly. She gave a trembling smile. "It was lovely to meet you. Take good care of my boys—both of them. *Adios.* Go with God...."

Tearfully Louisa rushed out the door. The elevator was gone so she ran down six flights of stairs. She barely made it outside the building, pushing open the door with a bang, before she saw the limousine pulling away from the curb with her husband and child inside it.

"Wait!" she screamed. The car stopped.

"Cutting it close," Rafael observed coolly, as she wrenched open the door.

Panting, she scrambled into the back beside the baby seat. She kissed Noah tearfully on his downy head then, as the car pulled away from the curb, she turned on Rafael.

"How could you do that to your own mother? She loves you! How could you be so cruel?"

"Now you know what I do to people who betray me," he said evenly. "It's taken almost twenty years, but I finally got justice for what she did to me. And to the father I never knew," he said coldly. He leaned forward. "To the airport."

"You are more heartless than I ever imagined," she whispered, suddenly frightened.

"I am not heartless." Abruptly Rafael leaned toward her in the backseat. He cupped her face with one hand. "For I am willing to forgive you, *mi vida,* for one mistake. One." He caressed her cheek. "But never cross me again."

"What do you mean?" she whispered, trembling beneath his touch.

"Never lie to me again. And I will allow you to remain my wife and raise our son. You will be honored and respected forever as my wife. But if you ever betray me again…"

Their eyes locked.

"If I do?" she whispered.

He abruptly pulled his hand away. He picked up the newspaper in his lap and unfolded it, creating a wall of newsprint between them. "Then you will lose everything."

CHAPTER TEN

You will lose everything.

A few weeks later in Paris, Louisa couldn't stop shivering in the cool spring morning as she sat outside at a riverside café overlooking Notre Dame across the Seine. Baby Noah was sleeping, tucked snugly into blankets in the baby stroller beside her. Louisa took another sip of coffee so hot and strong it scalded her tongue, but still she continued to shiver. Even in a black cashmere sweater, dark skinny jeans and knee-high boots, she felt cold down to her toes.

Closing her eyes, she turned her face toward the sun.

If Rafael ever learned what she'd just done…

I had no choice, she told herself fiercely. She couldn't allow him to so callously,

cruelly hurt his mother, not when his desire
for revenge would hurt everyone—grandmother, grandson, and most of all: Rafael
himself!

Just a few moments ago, Agustina had
been here at this café, sitting beside her.
She'd been so happy to see her grandson
again. A lump filled her throat. And Louisa
had finally learned the truth about Rafael's
past. She understood at last why his mother
had protected him all these years.

Rafael thought his mother was cold-
blooded and controlling. He was wrong. But
Louisa could not tell Rafael about his father,
any more than Agustina could. It would hurt
him too much. Louisa couldn't rip his heart
out with the truth. No matter how badly he
lashed out.

"Merci, madame."

Louisa looked up, blinking fast and trying
to smile at a waiter who left the bill. She put
down her euros, then drank the rest of her
tasse of hot black coffee. She glanced down
at her sleeping baby in the stroller, feeling
warmth and adoration swelling her heart.

"I'll find a way to break through to him,"
she whispered to her sleeping child. She'd

find a way to make him forgive his mother...
but how?

"Mi vida."

Louisa nearly jumped in her chair when
she heard Rafael's voice behind her. With a
gasp, she turned and saw him climbing out
of the limousine that had pulled to the curb.
"What are you doing here?"

He slammed the door closed then walked
toward her.

"Are you and Noah having a nice morning?" he said, smiling.

She rose to her feet so quickly all the
blood rushed from her head. "We were just
leaving."

She'd chosen this café in the *Quartier
Latin* because of its distance from their
penthouse, which was in the more exclusive
eighth arrondissement across the river. She'd
known he had a full schedule today, meeting
a new stockholder who owned a château to
the south of the city. She'd never imagined
he might drive right by the café. Of all the
quirks of fate...

She was suddenly sweating in the cool
spring air. If Rafael's car had driven past

this café just ten minutes ago, he would have actually seen his mother sitting beside her!

Their marriage, their building trust, could have been destroyed forever. She glanced down at her sleeping baby. Noah was so precious to her. Was she being a fool to risk a decent life, in hopes of having a happy family?

Rafael smiled at her. He looked so handsome in his dark suit and blue tie. His jawline was sharp and shaved, his eyes bright in the sunshine.

"Before I met with my stockholder, I went up to La Défense," he said. "Our new building is perfect."

"Is it done? Ahead of schedule?"

"Next week we'll start moving our people in. Then I'll take you to see it."

But would she still be his wife next week? Louisa's hands tightened on the handle of the stroller.

"Shall we walk back to the apartment?" he said.

Her eyes widened. "You have time? Now, in the middle of the day?"

Rafael shrugged. "It is a beautiful morning. I'll make time."

She swallowed. Of all the days she'd wished he would spend time with her, he was choosing now? Now, when she was racked with guilt and fear over what she'd done, bringing his mother secretly to Paris? She took a deep breath and tried to smile. "That would be lovely."

They walked together along the river. She gave him little glances. He'd been busy constantly with work since they'd arrived in Paris. He'd had time only to give his baby son a kiss each morning before he left—and when he came home late at night, he'd climbed into bed beside Louisa and made passionate love to her in the dark. But this was the most they'd spoken together in weeks.

In many ways, nothing had changed since the last time she'd lived in this city. She still based her whole world around Rafael Cruz, running his home and trying to gain his approval.

But in other ways, everything had changed. While she still oversaw the house, Rafael wanted her to spend her time as mother to their son—and as his wife. Which meant far too many shopping trips to the designer boutiques of the nearby Rue du Faubourg St-Honoré. In fact, in a few days, she would attend her first society ball on his arm.

The thought of attending the soirees she'd once organized for him, not as his house-keeper but as his wife, terrified her. The thought of facing all the various women he'd once slept with—and for all she knew, might someday sleep with again—made her ill.

She'd tried to create a loving home. But it wasn't enough, not nearly enough. He still didn't allow himself to be vulnerable. He still wouldn't allow himself to love either her or the baby.

Springtime in Paris was lovely. The flowers and trees were starting to come back to life. The baby was awake and chortling happily, kicking his feet in the air as Rafael pushed the stroller, by the time they reached the eighteenth-century building near the Champs-Élysées. Rafael owned the entire building, but only used the top two floors to live in. The floor beneath was for his body-guards and assistants, and the several floors below that were being used as office space until the new headquarters was finished.

As the elevator opened to their spacious

penthouse, Louisa took a deep breath at the beauty of the home and the view of the city. She could see the Eiffel Tower across the river. Even as housekeeper, she'd loved this home; and now she was not only its mistress, but the mistress of all Rafael's homes around the world.

But if he knew the truth about how she'd brought his mother to Paris and allowed her to spend time with Noah behind his back…

It was wrong. Louisa knew she shouldn't have done it. But he was so caught up in his ideas of revenge.

How could she ever make him forgive his mother, how could she ever get him to open his heart, without causing him irreparable harm?

A sudden thought occurred to her.

She could tell him the truth. Rather than wait for him to find out what she'd done— rather than avoid conflict, as she always had—she could take the bull by the horns and tell him all about it.

But the thought terrified her. No. She couldn't risk it!

Later that night, with their baby sleeping in his lavish nursery, a few hours after

Louisa had gone to bed, she felt Rafael climb in beside her. She always slept naked, as he preferred. Before she was quite sure whether she was dreaming, he was kissing her. She felt him on top of her, felt his body hot and hard against hers. Within moments, she was crying out her pleasure, and she heard his shout as he collapsed on top of her.

Afterward, he held her close in his arms in the darkness.

"I have a gift for you," he murmured against her skin.

She looked up at him in the shadows, her heart in her throat. "What is it?"

He purred in her ear, "Do you remember that private Greek island?"

How could she forget? Those were the happiest two days of her life. "Of course."

He kissed her temple and whispered, "I bought it for you today."

She sucked in her breath. "You—bought it?"

"Novros wasn't sure he wanted to sell." She heard his smile in the darkness. "But I convinced him."

"Thank you," she said softly. Her eyes

filled with tears as she held him tightly to her.

His hand moved toward her naked breast. "Anything for you, *querida*."

Anything?

Suddenly she knew she had to take the gamble. She wanted him to trust her. She didn't want to lie to him.

She loved him. He gave her everything she could want when it came to money, but so little of himself except his lovemaking, which was very inventive and satisfying. Now he'd given her an entire island, but it was still not enough. Not nearly enough.

She wanted *him.*

She wanted him to be the man he was born to be. The good, kind, loyal man she knew he had inside him, beneath all the calloused armor.

She entwined her fingers in his. "I have…a favor to ask you."

"A favor?"

Her teeth chattered. Was *favor* the right word to describe her request that he give up all thoughts of revenge, give up all his other women, and love her madly, as she loved him? "It's bigger than a favor."

"Ah. It takes more than a Greek island to impress you, does it?" He gave her a wicked half smile as he slowly moved his hand over her naked belly. "I will see what else I can do."

Though he'd just barely brought her to gasping fulfillment, she could feel that he already wanted her again. She felt the same. But before his touch could utterly distract her from taking the risk she must take, she put her hand over his own, stopping him.

"I have to tell you something," she whispered. "But I'm afraid."

"You can tell me anything," he said. "You've started to earn back my trust, *querida,*" he says softly. "I am glad of that."

A huge jolt went through her.

"I brought your mother to Paris," she blurted out. "I spoke with her at the café today." Her teeth chattered as she looked up at him and whispered, "You have to forgive her."

Rafael felt sucker-punched as he stared down at her.

"You brought my mother to Paris?" he said in a low voice. "You allowed her to see Noah?"

"Yes," she said, staring up at him, her hazel-brown eyes wide.

He ripped his hand away from her. As he rose naked to his feet from the bed, the world seemed to be spinning around him. "You disobeyed me."

She shook her head desperately. "I'm trying to save you!"

"Save me?" he ground out.

"Your mother loves you. You have to forgive her. She had a good reason for not telling you about your father!"

He sucked in his breath. "What was it?"

"I…I…" She hesitated. "I can't tell you."

His heart beat rapidly inside his hollow chest. There was a metallic taste in his mouth. "You betrayed me."

She grabbed his hand. "I could have lied to you. But I'm telling you the truth. I'm telling you now, rather than doing it behind your back. I—"

He was beyond listening. "I told you what would happen if you ever betrayed me."

She looked stricken, as if he'd just slapped her.

"Please," she whispered. "I was only trying to make us a real family."

He reached for his clothes and swiftly got dressed. "I told you what would happen," he repeated.

His words were cold and even, but inside, he felt sick.

He'd never thought she would betray him like this. He'd never thought he would have to carry through on his threat, but now he had no choice.

"But, Rafael," she whispered, "I love you."

"Love? All that you've proven," he said harshly, "is that every time I start to trust you, you stab me in the back."

"But I didn't—I told you the truth!"

"Yes, after the fact." How smug they must be right now, both the women in his life who'd conspired against him and made him look like a powerless fool in his own house! "I told you what would happen if you ever crossed me. Get out of my house. I'll be filing for divorce."

"I'm not leaving you, not now, not ever! But you can't treat your mother so shamefully, not when she is innocent of what you think she did—"

"She told you that, I suppose?" He sneered.

Louisa started to speak, then cut herself off. She took a deep breath. "She didn't have to tell me. I saw it in her eyes! She loves you, she would die to protect you. The same as I feel about Noah!"

"You'll have to love him from a distance," he said coldly. "Because I'm cutting you out of his life."

"I won't leave him—or you! If you want me to go, you'll have to throw me…" she flung her arms toward the wide tree-lined boulevard of the Champs Élysées "…out that window!"

"Very dramatic," he said acidly, following her gaze. "But your little act won't save you."

Now fully dressed, he strode out of the room and headed straight for the nursery. He heard Louisa rush to follow him, scrambling for a robe.

But Rafael didn't pause. He didn't stop. He simply collected his sleeping son from the crib. Noah immediately started to cry when he was woken up. His wails matched Louisa's screams and sobs as she abandoned her attempts at tying her robe and clutched wildly at his arm.

"No!" she screamed. "You can't take him away from me!"

He stared at her, feeling unmoved. Feeling absolutely nothing.

Or so he told himself.

"My lawyer will be in contact," he told her coldly. Ripping his arm away, he carried his son downstairs and had two words with the bodyguard in the small apartment below.

Louisa tried to follow him, but at his orders, his bodyguard held her back as Rafael left.

When Rafael arrived at his favorite hotel ten minutes later, he felt guilt and pain threatening to bubble up inside him as he climbed out of the chauffeured limousine. He pushed the emotion away. He told himself Louisa was no decent mother, no decent woman. She'd lied like all the rest.

She didn't deserve either Rafael—or their son.

By the time Rafael had checked into the penthouse suite at the hotel, and their part-time nanny had arrived after his assistant's frantic call, the baby still was crying. But even after the plump, motherly Frenchwoman had come up to the suite and taken the baby tenderly in her arms, Noah wouldn't stop crying. He cried until his little face was red.

And slowly, Rafael realized he was the liar.

Louisa had made him a liar.

Because he could not follow through with his threat. Damn her! He could not separate his son from her. No matter how she'd betrayed him, no matter if she deserved it, he could not see his son suffer without his mother.

Cursing her, cursing himself, he realized he would have to allow her access to their child. But their marriage was over, he told himself furiously. It was done. But as he reached for his phone to call Louisa, it rang in his hand.

"I never thought you could do something like this. Ever."

He frowned. *"Mamá?"* he replied slowly, almost not recognizing her voice.

"Louisa called. How could you take her baby from her? How could you! You are not the man I thought you were!"

He ground his teeth. Of course Louisa had called her! "What happened between my wife and me is no concern of yours."

"I am downstairs. I have something to tell you. Come down now."

"Why should I?" he said stiffly.

"See me this one last time, *mi hijo*. One last time before I go back to Argentina."

The phone clicked softly in his hands.

Rafael set his jaw. Fine. One short conversation would be a small price to pay to get the woman out of their lives forever. Rafael made sure his son was tucked away in the second bedroom with the French nanny, then went downstairs.

He found Agustina at the bar. He expected her to try to immediately look at him with timid love and a pleading smile, as she always had for the last twenty years.

But this time, she'd changed. She was no longer the soft, anxious woman he remembered. Her face was stern. She started speaking the instant he sat beside her at the darkened hotel bar.

"I've tried to protect you for all your life," she said without preamble. "But you are a man. At a certain point, no parent can protect their child. And now that I've heard what you've just done, I fear my protecting you has done you more harm than good." She pushed some pages toward him on the smooth polished dark wood of the bar. "Here."

A sneer twisted his lips as he reached for the pages.

The sneer soon dropped off his mouth as he read the old faded words. His eyes widened. He turned the page. He couldn't stop reading it. Five minutes later, he got the final stab in his throat when he read who'd signed the letter. His whole body felt cold when he finally looked up into the eyes of his mother.

"My father wrote this letter," he whispered, then shook his head, trying to get some warmth back into his body. "You told him you were pregnant with his child. And he told you to get rid of me."

His mother's eyes, so much like his own, looked at him steadily. "Yes. When I wouldn't, he sent me his gold ring. He said that was all I would ever get from him."

"Why?" he said over the lump in his throat. "Why didn't he want me?"

"He disliked children. And he'd never been

in love with me. I found out he'd never even been faithful to me." She took a deep breath. "I was so young. I had no way to support us. I went back to Buenos Aires and married the man my parents had wanted me to marry all along. Arturo said he would be a good father to you…but he did not follow through on that promise."

"But, *Mamá*," Rafael said slowly over the ragged, sharp pain in his throat, "why did you never tell me the truth? Why did you let me blame you for all these years? Why wouldn't you tell me my father's name?"

"You'd already suffered enough from having one father who didn't love you, and all those years you never knew why—until Arturo broke his word and told you the truth as he died." Her eyes went dark, then with a sigh, she dropped her hands into her lap and became the gentle mother he'd always known. "You were so young and so hurt. When you found out you weren't his true son, you imagined all these wonderful things about your real father. I couldn't let another father disappoint you. I couldn't let your heart be broken all over again."

Rafael sat back with shock in his chair.

Everything he'd thought was true—was wrong.

"I'm sorry," he whispered, turning to his mother. He put his hand over hers as he felt tears rise unbidden to his eyes. "I'm so sorry."

His mother smiled through her own open tears. "I'm sorry I couldn't give you the father you deserved," she whispered. "But you can be that father for Noah. You can give him the family I tried and failed to give to you."

Family. Rafael sucked in his breath.

Louisa.

All he could suddenly think about was what he'd done to his wife. The woman who tried so hard to love him.

"Does Louisa know?" he said faintly.

His mother nodded. "But she wasn't going to tell you. She didn't want to hurt you."

Rafael stared at her.

Louisa hadn't wanted to hurt him? Even when he'd done the cruelest thing possible to her, taking their child away, *she hadn't wanted to hurt him.* She'd been trying to protect him.

In spite of everything, in spite of knowing

his faults so well, Louisa truly loved him. The generosity and loyalty of her love took his breath away.

And this was how he'd treated her. She'd risked everything to tell him the part of the truth that would not hurt him, and he'd made her pay for it. She'd openly offered him her heart, not once but twice, and he'd wantonly ripped it apart, stomping on the pieces.

He stared blindly across the dark shadows of the exclusive bar.

"She'll never forgive me," he said.

He felt his mother's hand on his shoulder. "She will."

He looked up, no longer trying to hide the sheen of tears in his eyes. "How can I ever win her back? All this time I've thought I couldn't trust her. The truth is, how can she ever trust me?" He thought of his son crying upstairs. He'd done everything wrong from the start!

What could he do?

How could he ever make it up to her?

Louisa had tried to save his soul, and he'd repaid her by nearly destroying hers.

He loved her, he realized.

He loved her.

He'd been trying to fight it for years. Even as he'd told himself he just wanted her in his bed, or needed her skills in his home, the truth was that he'd loved her for years. Not just what she did for him, but *her*. Her smile, her gentleness, her feistiness. The way she looked all mussed in the morning. The way her eyes glinted with tenderness when she saw him across the room.

He loved her.

Clenching his hands into fists, he slowly rose to his feet.

He loved her. Even if it made him weak. Even if it made him vulnerable. He loved her, and he would make her love him.

He'd win this fight, or he would die trying.

CHAPTER ELEVEN

COLLAPSED on the floor, Louisa lay curled up on the priceless Turkish carpet. She'd run out of tears hours ago. The bodyguard who'd restrained her, Evan Jones, had seemed disgusted with his job that day, but he'd done as his boss had ordered, keeping her a virtual prisoner in the luxury penthouse.

After Rafael had left, Louisa had thought desperately of calling the police, then despaired. Rafael was, after all, Noah's father! So instead, she'd called Agustina, who'd cried with her over the phone. The older woman had promised to try to help. But what could she do, really?

Now, Louisa was numb. She shivered and shook in the cold, then rose and put on a T-shirt and pajama pants before her knees became weak and she collapsed back on the carpet. She stared up at the ceiling, staring blankly at a long, thin crack in the plaster.

She had cried until there were no tears left. She was numb. No: she was dead. When Rafael had left her, taking their sobbing baby with him, she had died inside.

Now nothing was left of her. She rose slowly to her feet. Opening the screen door, she went out to stand on the balcony. She stared out at the night. She felt the cold breeze against her hot face.

Across the river she could see the lit-up Eiffel Tower. She looked down into the darkness beneath the balcony. It would be so easy, she thought. So easy to end all the grief and pain with just one easy jump. She gripped the railing of the balcony, looking down at the street.

But she had to believe there was some chance she might see her husband and child again. She had to live in the hope someday she would hold them both in her arms.

She felt something cold and stinging against her face and realized she'd been wrong. She did, after all, have some tears left.

A hard knock sounded at the door.

Who could it be at this time of night? Who would the bodyguard even allow to come to her door?

For a moment, she didn't move. She stayed outside in the darkness. Then she heard something that ricocheted through her like a bullet.

Her son's cry.

With a choked gasp, Louisa ran inside, rushing across the apartment to fling open the door.

"Madame Cruz," she heard the elderly French nanny say, "your husband sent me…"

But Louisa heard no more. With a sob, Louisa took her son from the other woman's arms. She whispered words of love to her baby as she cradled him close, kissing his plump cheeks, his downy head, his fat arms. Noah hugged her desperately, and in a few moments, he ceased crying. He finally became calm, then abruptly fell asleep in her arms.

"Ah," the French nanny said tenderly, looking down at the baby in Louisa's arms. "*Enfin,* he sleeps."

For the first time, Louisa looked at her.

"What are you doing here?" she said, feeling like she was in a dream. "Why did Rafael send Noah back to me?"

The Frenchwoman shook her head. "I do not know, madame. But he wanted the baby brought to you immediately, even though it's the middle of the night." Stretching, she gave a discreet yawn. "If you please, I will go home now."

"But—he isn't demanding I send him back?"

"No," she replied quietly. "Monsieur Cruz said I was to make it particularly clear that he would never try to take Noah away from you again. He did ask if you would meet him for breakfast tomorrow."

Louisa's eyes narrowed. Meet Rafael for coffee and croissants, pretending nothing had happened, after all he'd done to her? Or worse—a preliminary meeting to discuss their imminent divorce? "No."

The other woman nodded with a rueful shrug. "I will relay your answer to him, madame. Now, if you will excuse me, I must go home to my bed."

Louisa cradled her sweet baby in her arms

all night. She slept slumped on the rocking chair, unwilling to be apart.

When she woke the next morning, she heard a knock on the door and answered it, her heart in her throat. She expected to find Rafael on her doorstep, demanding in his cold way for her to come with him to breakfast so they could meet with his lawyers.

Instead she saw a delivery boy staggering beneath the weight of a huge arrangement of roses, hundreds of them in every color.

"Flowers for you, madame," he gasped.

"Who sent these?" Then, behind him, Louisa saw the bodyguard smile, and she knew.

"Send them all back!" she thundered, and slammed the door.

But for the next three days, the gifts kept coming. No matter how firmly she sent them back, they didn't stop arriving. First there were the flowers, then after that came a team of manicurists and masseuses from the day spa. She received packages of clothes from all the top French designers. Handbags, exotic shoes, ball gowns. The capper was when a sports car in hot pink, with a big bow on the hood, was dropped off at the curb.

She refused them all.

Next came multiple deliveries from the finest jewelers in the city. Long ropes of priceless pearls. An emerald bracelet. A necklace of hundreds of sapphires. And finally: a diamond solitaire, as big as a robin's egg, set in platinum.

Louisa sent them all back.

For one long morning, her doorbell was silent. She spent her morning playing with the baby, baking a chocolate cake and trying not to think about Rafael. He wanted her back. That much seemed clear. But when was he going to stop sending her gifts? How long would it take to show him that her trust and forgiveness couldn't be bought?

Was Rafael ever going to come to her himself?

Then, the doorbell finally rang at last, and she braced herself to open it, knowing it would be Rafael.

Instead there was a messenger holding only a single rose—and a note.

I have something to tell you. Meet with me. Please.
Rafael

She took a deep breath. Then, she nodded. *"D'accord,"* she told the messenger. She was curious, she told herself. That was the only reason. That, and the fact that Rafael had actually written the note himself. She supposed she should be flattered!

The messenger nodded with a smile and said in French, "There is a car waiting outside to escort you and your baby to the airport. No need to pack anything for either of you. Monsieur Cruz, he has arranged for everything."

But Rafael wasn't waiting for them on his private jet. By the time the plane touched down at the private island, the Greek island she remembered all too well, Louisa could not pretend to herself anymore that she felt only curiosity. She wanted to see Rafael. No matter how she tried not to feel it, she missed him. Wanted him. And some part of her still wished he could love her. Though she now believed he never would love anyone.

But Rafael wasn't waiting for her on the tarmac. He wasn't waiting for her in the beautiful whitewashed house on the private island.

This was her island, now.

Had he changed his mind about meeting her here? Had he given up his pursuit? Was he just going to leave her in sole possession with the baby, the lonely queen of this island?

The house was empty. A strange disappointment went through her as she passed empty room after empty room.

She tucked her sleeping baby into the lovely elliptical crib she found in the newly decorated nursery. Closing the door softly behind her, she looked out at the orange and scarlet sunset. She walked across the empty house. She opened the screen door and went out on the terrace beside the infinity pool. Blinking back tears, she looked around her and remembered all the places where they'd once laughed, where they'd shared meals, where they'd made love. Past happiness surrounded her like the echo of ghosts.

Folding her arms, blinking back tears, she lifted her chin and stared out at the red twilight over the darkening blue sea. How had everything gone so wrong?

Her love hadn't been enough to save him.

It hadn't been enough to make him love her back.

But as she wept, Louisa suddenly heard a voice behind her.

"Forgive me."

With an intake of breath, she whirled around and saw Rafael. He was coming toward her. His figure was dark as a shadow in the deepening night. Only his eyes seemed like pools of light, gleaming at her with the intensity of fire.

"Forgive me," he said again. She was frozen by his gaze, unable to move as he came toward her. He took her in his arms. Holding her with his gaze, he brushed tendrils of hair back from her cheek. "I was so wrong."

She opened her mouth to speak, but he stopped her by placing a finger on her lips. He looked down at her, and she realized he had tears in his eyes as well.

"I love you," he whispered. "I love you, Louisa. You and only you. Since the day I took you to my bed, there has never been another woman for me. You are my lover. My friend. The mother of my child. Most of all—you are my wife. I love you."

She stared up at him, unable to breathe.

He lowered his head toward hers as his

hand stroked her face. "Can you ever forgive me?"

She shook her head, unable to speak.

"You sacrificed so much to protect me. I know everything now. My mother told me everything. I cannot live without you. Not just for Noah's sake, but for my own. Everything I am, everything that's good, is because of you."

"Oh, Rafael..."

He gave a ragged intake of breath. "I know you can't forgive me for taking Noah from you like I did. But I swear to you I will spend the rest of my life trying to earn your love back again. I can think of nothing but you. I want you, love you, need you and I always will...."

Louisa stopped his words with a kiss. When she pulled away, his handsome face was dazed with joy.

"Louisa..."

"I love you," she whispered tenderly. "And I never stopped loving you."

Pulling her back into his strong arms, Rafael kissed her fiercely beneath the dark sky, beneath the stars that fell into the deepness of the sea, twinkling light into eternity.

"We're engaged!"

Six months later, Louisa looked up from the poolside chair to see her sister holding out her left hand with a shyly joyful smile.

"Engaged?" Louisa exclaimed. "To who?"

Katie grinned back at Rafael's chief bodyguard. "All the times Madison and I have visited this island...I never thought I'd come back with a souvenir like this!"

"A husband is your idea of a souvenir?" Evan Jones said with a grin, then took Katie's hand in his own and said earnestly, looking into her eyes, "This time, I wasn't going to let her go back to Florida without me."

Louisa leaped to her feet, clapping her hands. "I'm so happy for you both."

All this time, she'd hoped her little sister would find true love...and now she had. She looked out toward the surf, where Rafael was playing with his little niece, Madison, and his son, Noah, who at fourteen months old was now running like crazy all over the sand as fast as his chubby little legs would carry him. "Does Rafael know yet?"

"Not yet," Evan said with a rueful grin. "We thought we'd better tell you first. We might need you to smooth things over. You know how Mr. Cruz hates staffing changes. He's not going to like getting a new chief bodyguard."

The three of them looked down at the beach. The sun was shining against the white sand. Baby Noah had picked up a little pail and shovel, and was running frantically in pursuit of his cousin Madison across the sand. Louisa heard her husband laugh as he scooped his son up, swinging him around. His deep laughter, along with the higher-pitched giggles of their son, was Louisa's favorite sound in the world.

"But it's too bad for him," Evan Jones said, turning back to Katie with a smile. "I've decided to quit the bodyguard gig to become a baker."

"So don't make Louisa do your dirty work," Katie said, nudging her new fiancé with her shoulder. "Go on, tell him you quit. You're the one with the gun!"

"Actually I don't have…" he started, then squared his shoulders. "All right. I'll do it."

He marched off toward the beach.

Once Evan was out of earshot, Louisa asked softly, "Are you sure about this? He's so different from Matthias…."

"I know." Katie looked at her, her eyes shining with tears of joy. "Evan is better than rich. He's an honest, loving man with a good heart."

"Not to mention brave." From a distance, Louisa saw her husband scowl at Evan, folding his arms as he received his now ex-bodyguard's news. She gave a little laugh. "Uh-oh. We'd better get down there!"

Once Louisa joined her husband on the beach, the situation was easily managed. Within three minutes Rafael was congratulating the man and wishing him all the best with a hearty clap on the back.

Afterward, Louisa took her husband's hand. Rafael turned to her, kissing her palm, looking down at her with eyes shining with love. Her heart turned over in her chest. Was any woman ever so lucky, to be so adored?

Then, with a laugh, she picked up their giggling baby and ran off into the surf to frolic. They were swiftly chased by the man she loved: her former boss, her forever lover, her beloved husband who'd had a good heart all along but just needed a little help to find it.

A housekeeper always knew just what to do. Just what her boss needed most.

And sometimes, Louisa thought, smiling as she looked back at the most handsome ex-playboy on earth, she knew it even before he did.